The high-velocity bullet ripped into his belly

The Phoenix Force warrior groaned. His body jackknifed from the burning pain in his bullet-punctured stomach. He fell to his knees. He tried to stand, tried to control his breath, tried to conquer the pain.

The molten lead inside him flared into a sunlike furnace. His strength faded rapidly. Nerve endings seemed to be scorched by fire. His body shrieked. It begged him to surrender consciousness.

And the thought came to the warrior again. It's the best way for men like us, yes? It is good to die with friends.

Mack Bolan's
PHOENIX FORCE

Mack Bolan's
ABLE TEAM

PHOENIX FORCE

The Black Alchemists

Gar Wilson

A GOLD EAGLE BOOK FROM

W RLDWIDE

TORONTO • NEW YORK • LONDON • PARIS
AMSTERDAM • STOCKHOLM • HAMBURG
ATHENS • MILAN • TOKYO • SYDNEY

First edition July 1984

ISBN 0-373-61312-1

Special thanks and acknowledgment to
William Fieldhouse for his contributions to this work.

Printed in Canada

1

Dead men stink. A cigar is one way to mask the stench.

Homicide Inspector Charles Darlington flicked the wheel of his Zippo lighter and held the flame to the tip of the panetela. Puffing, he shook his head with dismay.

In his twelve years with the San Francisco Police Department, he had lost count of the number of grisly bodies he had encountered. He had seen victims of multiple gunshot and knife wounds, their flesh shredded and soaked with blood. He had seen the remains of suicides splattered all over the pavement from high-rise falls. He had seen ghastly corpses fished from the bay, bloated and mutilated by weeks in sea water: fish feed. Putrid month-old corpses with eyeballs eaten by blowflies and the razor-slashed remains of whores cut to pieces by pimps were equally familiar to him. But never had he witnessed anything like the grotesque scene in the backyard of a quaint house in a quiet neighborhood on the outskirts of the city.

Darlington approached the medical examiner, Dr. Fred Bellows, who had been summoned to the scene.

"What can you tell me, Fred?"

"Not much until after the autopsy. Or should I say autopsies? Christ, what a mess! Twenty-three of them."

In the center of the yard a long picnic table was laid out as though a picnic had been in progress. Around it were littered the bodies. They varied from young to old: children, parents, grandparents. There was no blood except for some minor trickles from the nostrils of a few.

Yet these people had not died peacefully. Their bodies were contorted as though from great pain. Clawed hands clutched at throats and chests. Faces had been transformed into frozen masks of agony and horror.

As ambulance attendants milled about, Darlington and Bellows stepped back from the chaos of tangled bodies. "That's my count, too," Darlington said. "It's obviously a mass poisoning."

The portly balding doctor pulled off his wire-rimmed glasses and rubbed the bridge of his nose. "Nothing is obvious until after the autopsies," he said matter-of-factly.

"Bullshit, Fred. You figure the entire Merrill family all just happened to have heart attacks simultaneously? Even the kids? Come on."

"Merrill family, eh? What was this, a family reunion?"

"That's what the neighbors say. Apparently the Merrills came from all over the country for this Labor Day reunion. Neighbors heard a baby crying; it never stopped, so they decided to see what was wrong. That's when they saw this goddamn morgue.

The neighbors have a kid next door. They don't even know which Merrill couple it belonged to. One thing is for sure, there'll never be another family reunion for the Merrills.''

"Okay, Charlie," Bellows sighed. "I do have a preliminary opinion. I'd say it's almost certain these people are victims of cyanide poisoning."

"Cyanide?"

"Did you notice some victims had vomit drool on their lips? That pink froth is from their lungs. Christ, it's sickening. Do you smell bitter almonds? That's the aroma of cyanide. I'm sure of it, but I've sent in some smear samples for fast analysis so I can prove it."

"Jesus," Darlington whispered. "The stuff must have been in the food."

"Not necessarily. Cyanide can be inhaled or absorbed through the pores of the skin. It's also found in natural form in quite a few common plants and fruits. There's a small amount of it in peach pits, mountain laurel and lilies of the valley, to name a few."

"You think it's possible somebody added the wrong ingredient to the potato salad and poisoned the whole family by accident?"

"Some recipes include a lot of exotic herbs and such," Bellows said, "so it is possible. After all, it doesn't seem likely that the Merrill family was connected with the Mafia or Communist agents. Who would want to kill a bunch of middle-class American WASPs?"

"We don't know enough about the Merrills to rule

out anything yet," Darlington declared, watching as the first few bodies were bagged and taken away. "Nothing is definite about a homicide case until the case is closed."

"Yeah," Bellows said grimly. "I guess the only real fact we have so far is that the Merrill baby will have to find a new family. His old one isn't around anymore."

THE FOLLOWING MORNING Inspector Darlington read the medical examiner's autopsy reports of the first bodies. They confirmed his original suspicion. Members of the Merrill family had consumed a lethal amount of potassium cyanide. Undigested food in their stomachs proved it had been eaten.

Chemical analyses of food from the Merrill picnic table revealed how the cyanide had been introduced to the family. A can of cranberry sauce contained enough of the deadly toxin to kill a herd of elephants.

"Jesus," Darlington muttered, putting down the report. "Cyanide mixed with cranberry sauce. Why?"

He noted the brand name, although certain it had already been reported to the Food and Drug Administration. What the hell is safe these days, he wondered. Alcohol causes brain and liver damage. Everything from cigarettes to hair dryers is supposed to cause cancer. Half the food we eat is either high in fats or low in minerals. Even the air is full of toxic fumes.

But such a large dose of cyanide in the Merrill's cranberry sauce suggested a malicious, not accidental, poisoning. Darlington recalled stories of mercury poisoning in fish several years ago. An American journalist had won a Pulitzer for a story on the subject in Japan. The birth of some disfigured babies in Hiroshima and Nagasaki was commonly believed to be the result of the effects of radiation on the genes of parents who survived the atomic bombs that ended World War II. Mercury poison turned out to be the villain instead.

Thousands of fish caught in the waters off Japan had been contaminated by mercury fulminate dumped by paper mills along the coast. Victims suffered severe illness, sometimes death. The poison affected fetuses in their mothers' wombs and caused an assortment of gross deformities in the children.

More recently, fish were discovered with cancer tumors clustered throughout their bodies. Could cranberries be contaminated in a similar manner? How? From insecticides? Waste products in the soil? Something in the metal cans that held the sauce?

The homicide inspector did not dismiss any possibility.

He checked into the background of the Merrill family, finding no evidence of any connection with organized crime. None of the adult Merrills had ever been suspected of embezzling or of dealing in cocaine; none had been clients of loan sharks. A couple of ex-spouses seemed to be the closest thing to enemies any of them could have acquired over the years.

None of the teenagers had belonged to street gangs or had associated with militant political groups or crackpot religious cults. Except for a few traffic violations, one arrest for drunk and disorderly, and another misdemeanor for possession of a few ounces of marijuana, the Merrill family looked clean. There was no evidence to suggest anyone would have a reason to kill a single member of the family, let alone want to wipe out the whole tribe.

Darlington took a cigar from his pocket as he grimly considered what appeared to be the most likely explanation for the Merrill massacre. Someone in the family had purchased a can of cranberry sauce that had been purposefully sabotaged. The Merrills were random victims. They had been senselessly murdered by a sick bastard who had deliberately poisoned the food.

Such horrendous sabotage had occurred in the past. Sadists put razor blades in apples to give to kids on Halloween. Other warped lunatics slipped LSD into drinks of unsuspecting victims as a "joke."

Of course, the worst example was the so-called "Tylenol Killer." Not only had this fiend avoided capture, he opened the gate to copycat offenders. The public was justly horrified, aware that anyone could be a victim of such deranged sabotage. The tamperproof seals on pill bottles was a constant reminder that human monsters exist: demented beasts with vicious cunning who strike out at strangers.

"Oh, Christ," Darlington muttered to himself. "How do you catch somebody like that?"

The phone on his desk rang. He grabbed the receiver and put on his official voice, reciting his name and department in place of a hello.

"Charlie, this is Fred Bellows. We'll have some more Merrill autopsies completed later this afternoon, but we won't have them all finished for at least a week."

"I don't think there's any rush. We know what killed them anyway."

"Better make sure," Bellows said. "Besides, an autopsy is mandatory for every homicide."

"I know, Fred." Darlington spoke in a weary voice.

"By the way, are you going to contact the Houston police?"

"Houston? You mean Houston, Texas? What the hell for?"

"Haven't you heard the news? It was on the radio just a few minutes ago."

"What are you talking about?"

"There was another family killed in Houston," said Bellows. "Nineteen people died at a family reunion there. Cause of death: cyanide poisoning."

"Oh my God," Darlington rasped.

He did not curse. It was an expression of helplessness and a prayer of desperation.

"Oh my God...."

2

The President of the United States probably has the most demanding and difficult job in the world. His position requires incredible stamina and fortitude. Stress and fatigue take a heavy toll after four years in the White House.

Hal Brognola noticed how the President had aged since he was elected to office. The man seated behind the desk in the Oval Office had bags under both eyes and wrinkles that Brognola did not notice at their last meeting. Brognola did not envy the man. Responsibility and authority are heavy crosses to bear. He knew this from personal experience.

"Hello, Hal," the President said, glancing up from an open file folder on his desk. "Please, sit." With an outstretched hand he indicated a nearby chair.

"Thank you, sir," Brognola nodded, sinking into the chair.

"I'm not going to beat around the bush, Hal," the commander-in-chief declared. "I don't have the time. The fact is, I'm seriously considering dissolving your Stony Man organization."

"I was afraid you'd say that, sir," Brognola said with a sigh.

Stony Man had been created to utilize the unique abilities of virtually one man—Mack Bolan, better known as the Executioner. Bolan had proven his extraordinary combat skills and superior strategic talent during an incredible one-man war against the Mafia.

The Executioner accomplished the impossible. He not only survived, he actually defeated the Mob. His war had reduced the spread of organized crime to the level of crabgrass, needing only occasional trimming to keep under control. The government wanted to tap Bolan's warrior genius to combat the international threat of professional terrorism. Thus, Stony Man was formed.

Brognola had secretly assisted the Executioner in his previous war against the Mafia. Thus the federal officer had been chosen to serve as the middleman between the White House and Mack Bolan.

The Executioner was given a new identity: Colonel John Phoenix. Two incredible teams of antiterrorists were formed to assist him in his new war.

Stony Man had been a one-hundred-percent success against the twentieth-century cannibals. The Executioner, Able Team and Phoenix Force carried out mission after mission, each a stunning victory against the most ruthless and sinister of enemies. Yet terrorists proved more dangerous than even the Mafia. Political and religious fanatics will take incredible risks and plot the most outrageous conspiracies to accomplish their insane goals. Most have been associated with or controlled by the Soviet Union. The Kremlin's response to Stony Man was an elaborate scheme to neutralize Bolan and his people.

The scheme had been a partial success. Thanks to a cunning KGB frame-up, the Executioner had been labeled a dangerous, unstable renegade, and found himself hunted by virtually every law-enforcement and intelligence organization in the world. Now that Stony Man had lost its commander and chief agent, the future of this elite organization was at best uncertain.

"I wish you'd reconsider your attitude toward Colonel Phoenix," Brognola said.

"Bolan is no longer Colonel Phoenix," the President decided. "He made his decision. He proved that he has no respect for any laws or any form of justice except his own vigilante version."

"Bolan did what he felt he had to do, Mr. President," Brognola insisted as he chewed on the end of an unlit cigar. Weedy bits stuck to his teeth.

"That may be true," the President admitted. "But try to look at this from my position. How can we condone Bolan's actions? Maybe he was framed by the KGB, but no one can prove it and the Executioner's behavior appears to be nothing short of irrational."

"Can't you at least call off the dogs?" Brognola asked.

"That's out of my hands, Hal. Bolan is an outlaw. He's also a security risk. He knows too much. The man is a threat to our national security as long as he's alive. The Bolan matter is closed. All that remains is to drive the nails into his coffin."

"And you're planning to bury the rest of Stony Man as well?"

"We can't help wondering how reliable *any* of your supercommandos are, Hal."

"None of them has ever failed to accomplish a mission," Brognola declared proudly. "How can you question such results, Mr. President?"

"The three members of Able Team are old friends of the Executioner, correct? They helped him when Bolan was fighting organized crime years ago."

"And you think they may still be supporting Mack?"

"I think it's possible."

"Then you probably feel the same about me as well," said Brognola.

The President met his stare. "We haven't excluded that possibility either."

"You're wrong on both counts," Brognola told him. "What about Phoenix Force? Don't tell me you're suspicious of it as well."

"Bolan selected the members of the team."

"Phoenix Force comprises the best antiterrorists in the world," Brognola declared. "None of them is native-born American and none of them was associated with Mack Bolan until two years ago."

"I know Phoenix Force is supposed to be something of an American version of the foreign legion, specializing in semicovert operations," the President remarked. "That's just about all I know about them. I've checked with the CIA, the FBI and the Justice Department. None of them has any record of who belongs to Phoenix Force."

"Any section beyond Stony Man doesn't have clearance to receive that information."

"Does that include me?" the President asked.

"When you have a need to know," Brognola replied, "I'll tell you."

"I need to know something right now," the President said. "If I ordered you to dissolve Stony Man, would you do it?"

"I wouldn't have any choice, would I?"

"How stable is Phoenix Force?"

"Stable?" Brognola frowned.

"A couple of months ago they conducted a mission in Israel. This office didn't assign that mission, and I assume you didn't authorize it and order Phoenix Force into the field without notifying us."

"No, sir, I didn't," the Fed assured him. "But from what I know of the details, the mission was necessary...."

"One of the members of Phoenix Force is an Israeli, correct?"

"Yes, Mr. President."

"Is he more concerned about the national security of the United States or of Israel?"

"Both," Brognola declared. "With regards to that mission he was concerned about the well-being of the entire world. If he hadn't assembled the rest of Phoenix Force to deal with the terrorist plot he discovered in Israel, a full-scale war might have occurred in the Middle East."

"I'm not denying that," the President said. "But what if that incident had become public knowledge? It would look like the American government hired international mercenaries for clandestine operations against our allies. We'd be gutted. There'd be an overwhelming outcry from liberals that Phoenix Force was established in the first place, and an equally outraged scream from conservatives that we can't control its actions.''

"I believe most Americans would approve of what we're doing if they knew all the details," Brognola said confidently.

"You're not suggesting we make Stony Man a public matter?"

"Of course not. Tight security is mandatory for any clandestine organization. We have to keep secrets from our friends because there's no way to prevent them from reaching our enemies if we don't. It's just sometimes I think it's a goddamn pity that brave dedicated men never receive the credit they deserve. Of course, I won't have to be concerned about that any more if you've decided to dissolve Stony Man.''

"The nation is in trouble, Hal. We're desperate." The President closed the file folder on his desk.

"My people specialize in handling desperate situations, sir.''

"This one is different. Are you familiar with the rash of incidents recently involving the tampering of food, drugs and cosmetics?''

"Just what I've heard on TV and read in the newspapers. A couple of families in Frisco and Houston were killed with cyanide poison last September, wasn't it? Then some guy in Dayton was blinded by acid-laced eyedrops, and nine seniors in Tampa were hospitalized after using some sort of powder in a whirlpool at a health spa. Six died, if memory serves. Have there been other incidents?''

"Aren't those enough? The powder in the health spa contained sodium cyanide, by the way," the President stated, handing Brognola the file from his desk. "And that's just the tip of the iceberg, Hal."

"You mean these incidents are all related?" Brognola stared at the President.

"That's right," the commander-in-chief nodded. "It's probably the most insidious, cowardly conspiracy of all time."

The Fed flipped through the file, then looked up. "Who the hell are the Black Alchemists?"

"That's what you have to find out," the President replied. "Whoever they are, they claim to be responsible."

"This folder isn't very thick, sir. Is this all you have on these people?"

"You'll have to take the investigation from there."

"Our research department will do what it can, but Phoenix Force and Able Team aren't criminal investigators."

"Phoenix Force has done some successful investigative work in the past, hasn't it? From what little I've seen in those sketchy reports you send me, I'd say it did some pretty shrewd investigating in Germany and Japan before it located terrorist headquarters in both countries. Probably in Israel, as well."

"Phoenix Force is basically a strike team."

"Fine," the President stated. "When they find these terrorists who call themselves the Black Alchemists, that's exactly what I want them to do: strike and strike hard."

"Terminate?" Brognola raised his eyebrows. "We're not an assassination force."

"I didn't say that," the President told him. "But we can't allow this sort of thing to happen again. We've got to make certain the Black Alchemists are put out of business. Anyone who slaughters innocent people and expects this country to reward them by surrendering to blackmail will know they face swift and terrible retaliation. Naturally, I'd rather see these animals stand trial, but justice doesn't always come in a courtroom. Tell Phoenix Force to stop the Black Alchemists and use any and all methods necessary to accomplish its mission."

"And if it succeeds, you won't have any more doubts about Stony Man?"

The President rose, indicating the meeting was coming to a close. "If Phoenix Force succeeds, it will prove that it and the entire Stony Man organization is too valuable for dealing with matters that can't be handled via ordinary channels. To even consider dissolving your operations force under those circumstances would be out of the question."

"Understood," said Brognola, rising. "And thank you, Mr. President."

3

On the screen, two attendants briskly carried a stretcher from an ambulance into the building, the human cargo covered by a blanket. "Mrs. Elaine Simms was rushed to Cook County General Hospital following the incident," the anchorwoman for Chicago's Channel Five news reported. "Her condition is reported as critical."

Hal Brognola switched off the videotape machine and turned to the three members of Phoenix Force seated at the conference table in the War Room of Stony Man headquarters.

"That's the most recent incident," he said. "Mrs. Simms's face was eaten away by a couple of unlisted ingredients in her cold cream—ground glass and hydrochloric acid."

"Cristo," Rafael Encizo muttered. "What kind of vicious scum would do something like that?"

A muscular, handsome Cuban, Encizo was no stranger to "vicious scum." He had been captured by the Communists at the Bay of Pigs invasion and held in Cuba's most notorious political prison, where Castro's goons had interrogated and tortured him but could not break him.

Encizo escaped from the island hellhole and became a naturalized American citizen. An expert frogman, survivalist and combat veteran, he found use for his skills when the CIA recruited him for missions in Central America. Later he worked for an insurance company as an investigator, specializing in maritime claims.

An ideal choice for the elite antiterrorist unit, the Cuban warrior relished the adventure and the opportunity to strike out at the dark forces that he perceived were victimizing and enslaving people everywhere. When Phoenix Force was created, he finally found a home.

"They call themselves the Black Alchemists," Brognola explained, handing the men copies of the file he had been given at the White House.

"Is the President certain these incidents are connected?" Colonel Yakov Katzenelenbogen inquired.

A heavyset middle-aged Israeli who looked more like a college professor than a commando, Katz was one of the most experienced and deadly fighting men in the world. His career began when as a teenager in France he joined an underground resistance group against the Nazis. After the war, he saw little reason to remain in Europe as his entire family had died in Hitler's death camps, so he moved to Palestine, where he was soon involved in the war for independence. After the nation of Israel was established, Katz fought in the battles with her Arab neighbors; in the Six Day War his right arm was injured beyond repair and had to be amputated at the elbow. This did not prevent him from becoming an espionage agent with Mossad, Israel's main intelligence organization.

A brilliant linguist who spoke five languages fluently with smatterings of several others, Katz was recruited to serve as the team commander of Phoenix Force.

"He's sure," Brognola assured him. "The Black Alchemists aren't just capitalizing on a series of unrelated Tylenol-killer copycats to bluff their way through an extortion scheme. The White House received a cablegram from them that contained a list of stock numbers and other information to prove they had tampered with the products involved. The bastards even marked out letters and numbers on some of the labels. The FDA checked their claims. They aren't bluffing, Yakov."

"What do they want?" Keio Ohara asked.

The tall dapper Japanese was the youngest member of Phoenix Force. His quiet, gentle personality and polite manners concealed a fierce warrior, not unlike the fabled samurai knights of Nippon's past.

Though a seasoned veteran of eleven incredible missions with Phoenix Force, Ohara was still the least experienced of the five-man army. His special skills included a mastery of electronics and expertise in martial arts. A black belt in both judo and karate, Keio Ohara was a living weapon.

"They sent a list of demands," Brognola replied, consulting his copy of the President's folder. "The terrorists want $1 billion in cash. They've requested small denominations, unmarked bills, naturally. They are willing to accept diamonds as part of the payment."

"No demands that political prisoners be released?'' Katz asked. He deftly held a Camel cigarette between the curved hooks of the prosthetic device attached to the stump of his right arm.

"None," the Fed answered. "But they also want twenty-five-thousand M-16 assault rifles with ten times that in 5.5 ammo. And they want twenty LAW anti-tank rocket launchers plus one-hundred-thousand M-26 frag grenades."

"Insane! Sounds like a shopping list for a small army," Encizo burst out.

"That's unusual," Katz agreed, firing his cigarette with a battered old Ronson. "Most large terrorist organizations are controlled or at least supported by the Russian KGB. Moscow generally supplies them with plenty of weaponry."

"The Irish Republican Army has gotten more than half its weapons and explosives from sympathizers here in the United States," Ohara commented.

"Yeah, but that gravy train doesn't run so smoothly anymore," Encizo said. "The FBI conducted a big investigation of the Noraid organization a couple of years ago, and some of the IRA's American supporters stood trial for gun smuggling."

Brognola unwrapped a cigar. "But they were found not guilty on the gun-smuggling charges, weren't they?"

"True," said Katz. "But the incident certainly hurt the IRA's connections here."

"Where do the Black Alchemists want the money and hardware delivered?" Encizo asked. "That should give us some idea who's involved in this."

"They haven't specified locations yet," Brognola

explained, tossing his file folder onto the table. "They say that first they want to give us a few more examples of their ability to sabotage consumer products."

"Haven't they caused enough misery and taken enough lives already?" Ohara shook his head.

"Apparently they want to demonstrate that they can strike anywhere, anytime."

"Madre de Dios," Encizo muttered. "Anyone who doesn't live in the wilderness, eating roots and berries, will be vulnerable to those bastards."

"No wonder the President is so concerned about this matter," said Katz.

"He's also concerned about Stony Man," Brognola said dryly. "And he's still debating whether to keep us operational or not."

"Because of that business with Bolan?" Encizo asked.

Brognola nodded. "And your little adventure in Israel a couple months ago."

"It had to be done, Hal," said Katz.

"None of you bothered to notify Stony Man," the Fed declared. "We didn't even know you guys were in the Middle East until you returned and made reports. If Rafael hadn't been wounded, I wonder if you would have bothered to tell us anything."

"Of course we would have," Katz assured him. "You would have found out anyway. American intelligence and Stony Man both have sources in Israel. Right?"

"The President wonders if we've got any control of you men." Puffing on his cigar, Brognola exhaled a cloud of smoke. "Well, your mission in Israel is ancient history," he said. "Providing we can get into the President's good graces again. For the sake of the entire Stony Man complex, Phoenix Force had better be able to take care of these Black Alchemists."

"We intend to," Katz declared. "But we'd better have the entire team. Where are Manning and McCarter? I thought they arrived yesterday."

Gary Manning, one of the two missing members of the five-man army known as Phoenix Force, was a Canadian demolitions expert and rifle sharpshooter. A workaholic, he tackled every task with bulldog determination. The other absent member, David McCarter, was a veteran of the British Special Air Service, an ace pilot and an exceptional pistol marksman. He was totally fearless in combat and a true believer in the SAS motto: He Who Dares, Wins.

"Gary and David are in San Francisco trying to recruit a new man for the mission," said Brognola.

Encizo frowned. "A new man? You're not planning to put me on the shelf because of my leg?"

"Of course not," the Fed assured him. "But I want you to avoid direct combat this time, Rafael. I've seen the medical reports. Your ankle was virtually shattered by a bullet. You've got a steel pin in there and the bones probably haven't finished knitting yet."

"I'm fine," the man insisted. "I don't really need this cane. It's just sort of nice to have." He pointed the cane at a bulletin board on a far wall, then pressed a trigger hidden in its handle. The walking stick hissed like a serpent, and an eighteen-inch spear jetted from its shaft and slammed into the board, its steel tip buried in the cork.

"Jesus," Brognola whispered. "Where'd you come up with something like that?"

"I made it for him," Keio Ohara answered, a bit sheepishly. "Simple, really. I installed an extruded seamless aluminum tube in the cane. It's the barrel for the spear, which is powered by a cartridge of carbon dioxide."

"Sort of a concealed harpoon gun," Encizo remarked. "With my experience as a frogman and a spear-fisherman, this weapon suits me fine. So you can see I'm not exactly a helpless cripple."

"I didn't say you were," Brognola assured him. He glanced at Katz: the word "cripple" had apparently not upset the one-armed Israeli. Katz believed that only those people who don't adjust to their physical disabilities are handicapped. This most certainly did not apply to him.

"Hal has a valid point, Rafael," said the Israeli. "As you know, I also have a steel pin. It's in my left knee. Occasionally, the joint locks and I limp about for a couple days. Bloody nuisance, but I've never gone into combat when this happens. I have no right to risk the lives of my teammates by trying to prove how tough I am."

"As if any of us need proof." Encizo grinned. "All right. If I can't handle it, I'll stay out of action."

"To set your mind at ease, Rafael," Brognola said, "I'm not recruiting anyone to replace you. The fellow just happens to be uniquely qualified to assist in this particular mission."

"Who is he?"

"His name is Calvin James." The Fed tossed another file folder on the table. "There's the material we put together on him. Take a look."

"Are you certain he'll be willing to join us for something like this?" Katz asked, reaching for the folder.

Brognola grinned. "Read his file. I've got a feeling Calvin James has been waiting all his life for something like this to happen."

4

Sergeant Calvin James looked down. He had not intended to. He knew it would not make the task any easier to see the pavement twenty stories below. Both ends of the street had been blocked off by police barricades. Cops dressed in flak vests and riot helmets, resembling fat beetles, lurked behind what looked like toy squad cars from where James stood.

"Shit," he hissed through clenched teeth. "And I volunteered for this."

James and another SWAT officer, Don Rambo, carefully lowered themselves down the side of the Hilldale Pacific Bank building, their booted feet braced against the concrete wall, their gloved fists gripping strong nylon ropes.

The pair were not engaged in a training exercise. A gang of terrorists called the Arma de Liberación de Puerto Rico had seized control of the Hilldale Pacific office tower. The fanatics were holding one hundred five people hostage. They threatened to kill the executives, secretaries, computer operators, even the janitors, unless their demands were met within twenty-four hours.

But they could not agree on their demands.

They wanted "freedom for Puerto Rico"—whatever that meant.

They wanted the release of six ALPR members held in federal prisons for attempted destruction of several national monuments including the Statue of Liberty and the Washington Memorial.

They wanted $2 million to "finance the revolution against American imperialism."

Finally, the ALPR fanatics wanted a plane to return them to Puerto Rico. Later they changed this and demanded a flight to Cuba instead.

The San Francisco Police Department does not believe in rewarding criminals for assault, kidnapping and murder. Nor does it endorse surrender to blackmail. Its Special Weapons and Tactics unit had been created to deal with such situations. One of the best in the country, it was called in to defuse the ALPR before the hotheaded terrorists could explode.

Rescuing the hostages and capturing the terrorists would not be easy. The doors to the building were booby-trapped with explosives wired to the inside. Terrorist sentries were posted at several windows. Most of the ALPR hoods were armed with rifles equipped with sniper sights.

Only the roof appeared to be vulnerable and unguarded. A police helicopter had passed over the building and confirmed that no terrorists were stationed there. However, there was only one entrance, and the door was probably booby-trapped as well.

The SWAT team could have handled the situation in several ways. An outright siege would further endanger the hostages but of course they were already in extreme danger since the terrorists had already displayed their viciousness by slaughtering all security personnel in the bank. Due to the position of the booby traps, the only way SWAT officers could safely deal with them would be to blast the doors. This would alert the ALPR lunatics and probably result in a massacre.

SWAT commander Captain Reed decided the best choice of action would be to lower two men from the chopper to the roof. The pair would then go down the wall to an unguarded window and enter the building. From inside they would attempt to locate an entry for the rest of the SWAT strike force.

James and Rambo volunteered for this risky assignment. Reed had slight reservations about using either man for the job. Rambo was somewhat inexperienced and James tended to favor unorthodox methods. A tall lanky black man who had formerly been a medic with the SEALS in Vietnam, James was probably the best trained and most highly skilled officer in the outfit. Although Reed admired the sergeant's ability, he suspected Calvin James was better suited for seek-and-destroy missions in combat than civilian police work.

Another reason Reed had been reluctant to send James was that he was in demand elsewhere. Reed had received a radio message from the police commissioner. Apparently two agents from the Treasury Department had inquired at headquarters about "borrowing" James for some sort of special duty, probably with Justice or the American branch of Interpol.

Well, Reed thought. Uncle Sam can have Calvin James later. Providing he does not get himself killed now.

WHEN JAMES AND RAMBO reached the eighteenth-floor window of the Hilldale Pacific building, they were eager to climb inside. Although M-16 automatic rifles were slung across their shoulders and .357 Magnum revolvers holstered on their hips, these would be of little help if the men were discovered outside the building with their hands clinging to ropes.

Rambo braced his feet on the windowsill and removed a glass cutter from his utility belt. James slid a suction handle from his gear. The device was a foot-long plastic tube with a suction disc attached to each end. He clamped both discs firmly on the glass.

"I hope this doesn't trigger a burglar alarm," Rambo whispered as he moved the cutter to the pane.

"No sweat," James assured him. "I asked Reed about that before we left. This place has a silent alarm which sets off an alarm at the police station. It's already been deactivated."

"Man, you think of everything, Cal," Rambo said with admiration.

"Not quite," the black cop grinned. "I forgot to take a leak before we boarded the chopper."

Using the cutter, Rambo drew a large circle in the glass. As he rapped it with his knuckles, James pulled the handle gently until the round section of the pane popped loose. Separating it from the disc, James flung the glass to the deserted street below.

Reaching through the hole in the window, Rambo turned the latch crank, and the windows revolved to their open position. Gripping the rope, he walked along the wall, then slipped feetfirst into the opening.

James prepared to follow his partner inside when

he saw another figure suddenly appear in the hallway within. A man dressed in an Army-surplus field jacket decorated with a Puerto Rican flag and clenched-fist emblems for shoulder patches quickly seized Rambo from behind and grabbed his hair, yanking his head back. Then the terrorist slashed a Bowie knife across Rambo's exposed throat. The lips of the wound curled back and blood geysered across the officer's dark-blue uniform and onto the floor. Then Rambo collapsed, the fire gone out of his eyes.

"Son of a bitch," James hissed as he grabbed the rope in both fists. Snapping both legs out to full extension, he swung away from the building, then swung back through the window and launched himself at the terrorist. The killer turned to see the soles of a pair of boots rocketing toward him. Before he could react, James slammed the heels of both feet into the Puerto Rican's face.

The kick sent him hurtling into a wall. The knife fell from his fingers as he slid, falling to one knee. Blood oozed from his crushed nose and pulverized mouth, yet his eyes were blazing with rage.

His face a stern ebony mask of determination, Calvin James unhesitatingly approached his opponent, who suddenly stood upright and reached for a snub-nose revolver in his belt. James hissed a *kiai* and swung a *chok-do* kick to the man's forearm. The edge of his boot struck the ulnar nerve and rendered the limb numb with pain. The terrorist's fingers refused to close around the grips of his gun.

James's arm flashed in a cross-body stroke. The side of his hand crashed into the man's throat, delivering a karate chop that caved in his thyroid cartilage and closed off the trachea. The terrorist stumbled and fell, both hands clamped to his ruined throat. He twisted and gurgled for several seconds, then slumped to the floor, dead.

"Hijo de la chingada!" an angry voice snarled.

James looked up to see the shape of another terrorist bolt from the corner of the corridor. He began to unsling the M-16, but the other man closed in too fast. The blur of a rifle stock whirled at James's face. The SWAT pro tried to duck. Walnut smacked into his cheekbone hard. Pain shot through his skull and the hallway turned into a spinning maze of color.

Calvin James found himself on the tile floor. A boot sent his M-16 sliding beyond arm's reach. A sinister figure hovered over him. A bearded face, capped by a brown beret with a yellow star insignia, glared down at him.

"Negro cochino," the terrorist rasped as he pointed a lever action .30-.30 Winchester at his chest.

5

The gunman's head abruptly snapped forward. Calvin James heard the harsh metallic cough of a silenced pistol and watched the terrorist's face explode. Blood and brains spat from a cavity where the Puerto Rican's nose had been a moment before. The deer rifle fell from his grasp. A second later, his corpse collapsed on top of it.

Two men stood at the end of the corridor. They were dressed like a pair of sports writers. The taller of the two wore a wrinkled brown jacket and a black turtleneck shirt with a cloth cap pulled over his forehead. His shorter, muscular companion was clad in a green jacket, checkered shirt and a black wool cap.

Both men also wore skintight rubber gloves, dark mustaches and eyeglasses with tinted lenses. Their wardrobe served as an effective disguise. James realized if he was asked to identify either man, he would only be able to make a general description of height and build.

The most impressive feature about them was their arsenal. The tall guy in the brown jacket held a 9mm Browning Hi-Power in a two-handed Weaver combat grip. A ribbon of smoke curled from the muzzle of a ten-inch suppressor attached to the muzzle of the pistol. There was little doubt who had shot the terrorist in the back of the skull.

In addition to the Browning, the guy in brown also had an Ingram M-10 machine pistol hanging by a long sling next to his right hip. The Ingram was also equipped with a black Sionics suppressor.

The dude in green, resembling a lumberjack, looked equally formidable. He held a Heckler & Koch MP5 SD3 machine carbine in his big hands. The sliding stock was fully extended and the foot-long sound suppressor fixed to its muzzle. The guy also carried a backpack strapped to his brawny shoulders.

"Bloody hell," the man in brown growled, revealing a British accent. "The bastards killed his partner."

"We got here as soon as we could," the other sighed. "Are you all right, Sergeant James?"

"Yeah," the cop replied, rubbing his bruised cheek. "Thanks to you two."

"Tough bloke," the tall Englishman in brown commented. "A butt-stroke like that would have knocked most men out cold."

"Hey," James began, scrambling to his feet. "Who the hell are you dudes?"

"For now you can just call us Mr. Green and Mr. Brown," the Briton replied.

"Uh-huh," James said dryly. "I guess I tell you apart by the color of your jackets. Right?"

"You guessed it," the man in green nodded.

"Cute," the SWAT sergeant remarked. "Well, if you won't tell me who you are, maybe you'll explain how you know who I am and what you're doing in here.''

"We'll discuss that later," the Briton told him. "Right now we'd better take care of the rest of these terrorists."

"I'll radio my unit commander..." James began.

"The hell you will," Mr. Brown snapped. "We don't need them mucking about when we've got a job to do."

"The San Francisco SWAT team is damn good," Mr. Green added, trying to soften his partner's sharp remarks. "But they're still policemen and that means they're restricted in certain ways that we're not."

"Goddammit," James said angrily. "Who the hell are you guys?"

"A couple of chaps who managed to enter this building despite the police blockade, terrorist sentries and explosives rigged to the doors," Mr. Brown said. "Now, if you don't think we know what we're doing, please say so."

"Okay," said James reluctantly. "Let's hear your plan."

"Just get your rifle and follow us," Mr. Green replied. "You'll know what to do."

Before James could argue, Brown and Green turned and headed down the corridor. The black cop cursed under his breath and followed them to a door at the end of the hall. Then James noticed the corpse of another ALPR goon slumped in a corner. A deep gash had been delivered to his neck. The terrorist had a terminal case of ring around the collar...in blood.

"What did you do?" James whispered. "Cut his throat with a straight razor?"

"Wire garrote," Mr. Green answered simply.

"Jesus," James rasped. "How many of these guys have you killed?"

"Don't worry," Mr. Brown replied as he unslung the Ingram from his shoulder. "There's still a whole roomful of terrorists left."

"And you want to take them on without any back-up?" James clucked his tongue with disgust. "What is this grand-slam-for-glory shit?"

"Look," Brown hissed. "We don't have time to argue. A lot of lives are in danger."

"Including our own," James muttered.

Mr. Green ignored the debate. The muscular man with the poker face slipped off his backpack, opened it and extracted an odd weapon that resembled a bulky pellet pistol. Green handed the gun to Brown.

"What's that?" James asked.

"A Bio-Inoculator," Green replied, taking an identical pistol from the pack. "It's usually used to tranquilize large game animals."

Mr. Brown eased the door open: it led to a flight of fire stairs. The Briton held the Ingram in his left fist and the B-I pistol in his right as he moved to the steps. Green followed. James brought up the rear, his M-16 ready.

Halfway down the stairs, Brown spotted an ALPR sentry armed with a Winchester riot gun in a corridor below. The guard gasped in surprise and worked the pump to chamber a shotshell. The Englishman snap-aimed and triggered his B-I pistol.

The tranquilizer dart hissed as it shot from the muzzle of the Bio-Inoculator. The sentry staggered from the impact of a steel hypodart in the upper torso. Green immediately fired another dart into his chest. The sentry dropped his shotgun and collapsed with a choking groan.

"What drug did you use?" James whispered.

"Thorazine," Green replied. "One hundred fifty milligrams in each dart."

"That's three hundred total," James whistled. "Dude's gonna be feeling pretty sick when he comes around. Probably suffer from jaundice. Maybe dyspnea and dyskinesia as well."

"Glad to see you've kept up with your biochemistry," Green remarked.

James started. How the hell did these guys know he had studied biochemistry? But he didn't ask, knowing they probably wouldn't tell him anyhow.

Brown descended the stairs and hastily scanned the corridor. He waved to the others to join him. "No more sentries," he whispered. He dragged the unconscious terrorist to a corner and pulled two plastic riot cuffs from a pocket. "We've been lucky. Haven't had to make much noise so far."

"That'll end pretty soon," Green declared. "The main objective is just around the corner."

"You mean that's where they're holding the hostages?" asked James as Brown bound the sentry's wrists and ankles. "How do you know that? Or is that another secret?"

"We peeked through a window with an infrared

imaging telescope,'' Green said. ''The terrorists have herded the prisoners to the west wing and they're holding them in an office section. Two sentries are guarding the captives with Thompson submachine guns. There are more terrorists in the section, but we'll have to take care of those two first.''

''I just hope none of your SWAT sharpshooters blast us when we enter the room,'' Brown commented. ''I'm sure your people have riflemen trained on the terrorists at the windows.''

''That's right,'' James admitted. ''Figured we'd probably have to take them out fast when we launched a siege on the place.''

''Not a bad idea,'' Green agreed. ''Except the other terrorists in the section would still slaughter the hostages.''

''We're here now,'' James remarked. ''I guess we're going to handle the siege ourselves. Maybe I should tell my commander and have him order the SWAT snipers to hold their fire.''

''What do you think, Mr. Brown?'' Green asked.

''Calvin James here seems to trust us,'' the Briton replied. ''Let's see if we can trust him as well.''

''Okay,'' Green said, nodding to James. ''Go ahead.''

The SWAT sergeant removed his walkie-talkie and pressed the transmit button. ''Captain?'' he spoke into the radio. ''This is Cal.''

''Read you, Cal,'' came the SWAT commander's voice. ''We were getting worried about you guys.''

''Rambo bought the farm. He's dead. But so are some of the ALPR terrorists.''

"Jesus," Reed's voice rasped. "What the hell is going on in there?"

"I've got some help. We're about to hit the main office section to rescue the hostages."

"What? Who's in there with you?"

"Never mind," James insisted. "Just tell the marksmen to hold their fire."

"Cal, have you flipped your Afro?"

"Gotta go, Captain," James said quickly. Then he switched off the talkie. "Let's do it."

MR. GREEN OPENED HIS BACKPACK and retrieved three black metal tubes, each less than a foot long, each with a dial attached to one end. To James the objects resembled sophisticated pipe bombs with egg timers welded to the metal.

"These are stun grenades," Green explained, as he and Brown returned their B-I pistols to the pack. "I designed these for situations like this, where high explosives might injure innocent bystanders. They're better than the Schermullys."

"When we blow the doors," Brown instructed, unscrewing the sound suppressor from his Ingram, "I'll take care of the watchdogs guarding the hostages, you chaps concentrate on the rest of the bastards and cover my arse. Agreed?"

"I'm going to have a hell of a time trying to explain this mess," James muttered as he unslung his M-16 and flicked the selector switch to semiauto.

Green moved to the corner and peered around the edge, exposing only one eye. There were a pair of glass doors at the end of the next corridor. Beyond that the demolitions expert could see only some desks topped by IBM typewriters and computer consoles, and a row of filing cabinets along the wall. Against the end cabinet leaned an ALPR terrorist, a pump shotgun held loosely in his fist.

The man in the green jacket slipped two stun grenades into pockets inside his coat and unslung his H&K machine carbine. He calmly set the timer to the third stun grenade and watched the dial tick toward zero. Then he nodded and tossed the tube at the doors.

There was a huge flash followed by a clap of thunder that reverberated within the corridor. James expected the walls to tumble from the explosion, but they did not. Green and Brown immediately dashed for the door; James followed.

In fact, the explosion had merely shattered the glass doors and rattled the occupants within the office. Before they could respond to the surprise attack, Brown leaped through the ragged entrance and snap-aimed his Ingram at the two ALPR flunkies guarding the hostages.

Swift and ruthless, the Briton opened fire, blasting 3-round bursts at the heads of two terrorist sentries. Their skulls popped like blood-filled balloons. Both were dead before either had time to squeeze a trigger.

"Down, goddammit!" the Briton shouted at several hostages who had been too startled to duck. Most of the captives were already hugging the floor.

Green entered immediately behind Brown, his H&K aimed at the gunmen at the opposite end of the office section. Their attention was still locked on the bold Briton who had plunged into the room like a machine-gun-toting Errol Flynn. The H&K chattered a furious volley of jacketed 9mm slugs that smashed into the chests of three ALPR thugs. Kicked backward by the force of the high-velocity missiles, they fell against office furniture and tumbled gracelessly to the floor.

At the doorway, Calvin James watched the Puerto Rican killers crumble under the relentless gunfire. Whoever Brown and Green might be, they were superb combat professionals. The pair operated with cool efficiency, daring nerve and flawless teamwork.

There was no time to further admire the skills of his mysterious partners: a head with a brown beret popped up behind a desk, then shoulders appeared as a terrorist raised a Mini-14 rifle.

James used the doorway for a barricade support and braced the barrel of his M-16 against the jamb. Just like basic combat training in marksmanship, he thought as he squeezed the trigger. A 5.56mm bullet pierced the terrorist's forehead. The ALPR goon slumped behind the desk and his Mini-14 clattered to the floor.

Green and Brown continued to display their survival expertise. The pair had scrambled to cover behind a couple of large metal desks: the terrorists did likewise, and recklessly fired in the general direction of the two warriors. Bullets punched through steel, seeking living beings. Brown and Green conserved ammunition, waiting for a clear target to appear.

James flicked the M-16 selector to full auto and

loosed a burst of 5.56mm rounds at the fanatics. The terrorists cried out in fear and ducked as bullets ricocheted against metal, kicking jagged splinters in all directions. Two ALPR members screamed when projectiles found flesh. James dashed to the closest desk and crouched behind it.

"Bloody good, Calvin," the Briton declared with a wolfish grin. "Now be ready. The bastards are going to jump us any second."

James was puzzled by Brown's remark until he glanced over at Green. The demolitions expert had drawn another modified stun grenade from his jacket. He set the timer and hurled the tube at the terrorists' position.

Two seconds later came another stunning but harmless blast. The mangled corpse of an ALPR terrorist was thrown over a desk. Other gunmen panicked and bolted from cover. Brown and James were ready for them. The Ingram and M-16 chattered twin streams of full-auto destruction. Bodies tumbled into desks and dropped in the aisles.

Three ALPR members darted for a door leading to another room. One of them pointed a sawed-off double-barrel shotgun at the raiders. A salvo from Brown's Ingram threw the gunman backward into his two comrades, riddling his chest with bullet holes.

"*Cristo!*" a Puerto Rican exclaimed. "Don't shoot no more, man!"

The remaining two terrorists threw down their weapons and raised empty hands in surrender.

"Face the wall," James ordered. "Spread-eagle. You guys know the routine."

"Watch it," Green warned. "These aren't just a couple punks who tried to stick up a liquor store."

"I'm not going to shoot down unarmed men," James declared as he approached the surrendered terrorists.

"Bloody policeman mentality," the Briton growled to his partner. "Better cover him, Gary."

Calvin James held his M-16 ready as he drew closer to the terrorists. They stood with their hands against the wall, their legs spread wide. James suddenly noticed a movement from the corner of his eye. He turned sharply to see an ALPR killer emerge from the shelter of a desk with an Army Colt .45 Auto in his fists.

The gunman had the drop on James. He had him cold as a corpse in a glacier. James knew he could not move his M-16 fast enough to aim and fire before the terrorist pulled the trigger of his Colt. Yet, the SWAT officer had no other choice: better to die like a ram than like a sheep. He whirled desperately to face his assailant, hoping to take the killer with him to the grave.

The terrorist's face suddenly became a mass of crimson pulp as a trio of 9mm slugs slammed into the side of his head. His skull burst, splattering brains over the keyboard of a word processor.

"*¡Bastardo!*" a Puerto Rican snarled.

James turned to see one of the terrorists no longer against the wall. The ALPR fanatic glared at the police sergeant as he dragged a .380 caliber Beretta backup automatic from his belt.

Calvin James lunged forward and rapidly lashed

the barrel of his assault rifle across the terrorist's wrist. The Beretta was chopped from the man's grasp. Instantly, the SWAT cop followed through with a fast butt stroke to his opponent's face and a vicious snap-kick to the groin. The ALPR stooge clutched both hands to his battered genitals and wilted to the floor.

The other terrorist abruptly leaped forward, seized the receiver of James's M-16, and desperately tried to take control of the gun. James did not waste time playing tug-of-war. He stomped a boot heel into the man's instep.

Bone crunched; the terrorist howled in pain but held on to the rifle. James clung to the M-16 with his left hand while his right delivered two trip-hammer-fast punches to the killer's mouth and nose. Before the dazed terrorist could decide whether to hold on to the gun or release one hand to defend himself, Calvin James struck twice more.

He swung a horizontal elbow stroke to the thug's jawbone and whipped a karate back fist to his right temple. His opponent's eyes crossed, and he uttered a weary sigh as if relieved that the conflict was over. Then he fell into an unconscious lump at James's feet.

"That's the last of them," Brown announced.

"We've got to get out of here," said Green.

"Wait a minute," James urged as he finished binding the wrists of the two dazed terrorists with riot cuffs. "I want some answers, dammit!"

"All right," Green agreed. "Give the sergeant a hand, Mr. Brown."

"I've taken care of these guys. . ." James began.

He barely saw a blur of motion. Mr. Brown was good. He quickly jabbed his stiffened, calloused fingers into the cop's mastoid. Briefly James felt a sharp pain behind his left ear, and the world became a big soft shadow of oblivion.

6

"How's your head?" a voice echoed from the end of a long black tunnel.

Sergeant Calvin James shook it experimentally. A dull pain throbbed at the back of his skull. He had been slugged before. The sensation was not unlike waking up with a megahangover. He opened his eyes slowly.

He was in the back of a van. An electronic device resembling a stereo set was mounted on a shelf. A pipelike object that reminded James of a periscope extended from the ceiling. James could see nothing else in the shadows except the heads and shoulders of two men seated in front of him.

"Here's an ice pack," a familiar British voice declared. "Sorry I had to cosh you, mate."

James accepted the cold blue bag from the shadow. "You hit hard, fella."

"Wanted to put you out with the first blow."

He pressed the ice pack to his skull. "Have either of you ever heard there's a law against assaulting and kidnapping a police officer?"

"Sorry for the extreme action," came the voice of Mr. Green. "All we planned to do was talk to you, but when we learned you were in that building we figured this would be a chance to see how you handle yourself in combat.''

"And to see how well you'd take to our methods," the Briton said, chuckling. "You did quite well, by the way."

"Who are you?"

"We're members of a top-secret organization that specializes in dealing with international terrorism."

"CIA?"

"I said *top secret*," Green told him. "You won't read about us in *Time* or *Newsweek*. We don't have security leaks or defectors. My partner and I were sent to try to recruit you for a mission."

James stared at the humanoid shapes. "Why me?"

"Because you're an ideal choice for this mission," Green answered. "As I recall, you were born in Chicago. A rough neighborhood on the south side. You joined the Navy at the age of seventeen. You were trained as a hospital corpsman. The elite Seals took an interest in you when they learned of your intelligence, medical skills and physical prowess. They were especially impressed by the fact you had learned fluent Spanish from Mexican Americans in Chicago."

"And you acquired considerable skill as a knife fighter while you were a lad as well," the Briton added.

"In addition to such unique Seals training as underwater combat and parachuting," Green recited. "You also took special naval classes in French, Vietnamese and medicine. Then you went to Vietnam for two years. Saw a good deal of combat and operated with a unit attached to the Special Observation Group—a CIA cover organization."

Brown continued, "You were wounded during the last SOG mission. You received an honorable discharge under medical conditions. You were also awarded several decorations for courage and devotion to duty."

"Wonderful," James muttered. "I've been kidnapped to be a guest on 'This is Your Life.' "

"Just let us finish," Green insisted, "and let's see if we have this right. Most of your family is dead. Your father from a heart attack in 1978 and your mother at the hands of muggers in 1980. Your older brother is a doctor and presently lives in Indianapolis. Your younger brother was a marine in Nam. Listed as killed in action."

"Missing in action," James corrected. "Waldo's body was never found. He might still be alive."

"MIA," Green confirmed. "And your sister is dead."

"Yeah," James whispered. His stomach twisted in recollection.

"You moved to California to study medicine and chemistry at UCLA on your GI bill," Green said. "But after the deaths of your mother and sister, you switched to police science. Later you joined the San Francisco Police Department. Your unique background made you an ideal recruit for its SWAT section. That pretty well brings us up to date."

"How did you get this information?"

"We've got our sources," Brown replied. "You might be interested to know that the FBI, Justice Department and even the CIA have files on you. They've all considered you for possible recruitment, but you have a rather unpredictable nature and you favor unorthodox tactics. Government blokes get nervous about such traits."

"But it doesn't bother you dudes?" James asked.

"We're not part of a bureaucracy," Green remarked. "We're sort of a maverick organization. We're assigned missions, but how we handle them is up to us."

"You were pretty impressive fighting the ALPR," James admitted.

"Those ragtag hoods were candy," the Briton said, chuckling. "They're unruly school kids compared to *real* professional terrorists."

"Since you wanted to talk to me alone," James asked, "what would you have done if Officer Rambo hadn't been killed?"

"Tranquilized him with a hypodart," Brown answered. "We don't hurt innocent bystanders or chaps on our side, but we hit the enemy with everything we've got. We get the bloody job done, Calvin."

"And we can use your help," Green added.

"What if I refuse?"

"Then you're free to go," Green replied. "The police commissioner thinks we're with the Treasury Department. Nobody can prove anything, so our organization will remain safe enough."

"What about my job with the SWAT team if I accept?"

"Officially you'll be away on a special assignment with the Justice boys," Brown answered. "Everything will be covered."

"I must be crazy," James sighed. "I accept. What's the name of this supersecret outfit I've been drafted into?"

"Everything will be explained when we arrive at headquarters," the Englishman announced. "A plane is waiting for us at a private airstrip. Let's be on our way."

"You mean *now*?" James whistled softly. "Man, you dudes don't waste any time."

"There are too many lives at stake to allow for that luxury," Green replied grimly.

SIX HOURS LATER Calvin James met Hal Brognola and the men of Phoenix Force in the Stony Man War Room. Mr. Brown and Mr. Green had already revealed their true identities. The daring Briton in the brown jacket was David McCarter, and the meticulous demolitions expert in green was Gary Manning.

Brognola shook James's hand and warmly welcomed him to the team. His manner toward Manning and McCarter was considerably less friendly.

"He's still wearing his SWAT uniform," the Fed whispered out of James's earshot. "What sort of crazy stunt did you two pull back in Frisco?"

"That's a bit difficult to explain," McCarter replied. "But we'll write a detailed report for you if you like."

"I have a feeling the fewer details I know the better off I'll be," Brognola muttered. "Sit down and we'll bring everybody up to date about this Black Alchemist business."

Brognola briefed James about the sabotage and

blackmail conspiracy and the mysterious terrorists who called themselves the Black Alchemists. Then he produced a computer printout sheet.

"Less than half an hour ago," he said, "we received this message via our computer complex. Calvin doesn't know Aaron Kurtzman, our computer wizard. He was seriously injured a while back and confined to a wheelchair, but 'The Bear' is still the best console jockey in the business. Aaron runs the best computer system in the world. We've got links with every major intelligence network and law-enforcement agency in the free world, not to mention numerous police departments throughout the United States."

"Do they know you're tapped into their computers?" James asked.

"They don't even know we exist," the Fed answered. "Some police departments think we're the FBI. The FBI thinks we're Interpol and Interpol thinks we're CIA. Of course, we've got a lot of covert taps they're completely unaware of. The people in charge of gathering data for Kurtzman all think they're working for one of the major intel organizations. We've even got a tap on the Soviet Embassy in Washington D.C., installed by a disillusioned KGB case officer who thinks he's working for Yugoslavian Intelligence."

"Spying on the spies." James whistled. "Quite an operation you guys put together."

"We like it," Rafael Encizo said with a grin.

Brognola held up the computer printout. "This sheet informs us that the police in Springfield, Illinois have arrested an employee of the local branch of the Blue Label Corporation. The accused, calling himself Donald Anderson, was filling tubes of toothpaste on an assembly line. Son of a bitch was caught slipping in small doses of a liquid substance that turned out to be hydrogen cyanide.''

"Sounds like he might be working for the Black Alchemists," Yakov Katzenelenbogen commented, reaching for his cigarettes. "What's Kurtzman's source?''

"FBI linkup," Brognola answered. "The Springfield cops wanted a rap sheet on Anderson. Turns out the little bastard was using a phony ID, social-security card and driver's license. His fingerprints identified him as Howard Jenson. He's been busted a couple times. Petty crimes mostly. Has a heroin habit. Served two years in the Ohio State Pen for armed robbery. Got out on parole in 1982 and skipped out of state. Nobody knew anything about his whereabouts until now.''

"Aren't we going to work with the FBI and the local police in Springfield?" James asked.

"Not in the conventional manner," Keio Ohara replied.

"Oh, we've worked with a number of intelligence and law-enforcement agencies in the past," Encizo interjected. "Kompei in Japan, the BND and GSG-Nine in West Germany, the Justice Department here in the States. But we have to be careful about how we operate with any of them.''

"Ironically," Katz said, "although we're working for the interests of the United States, we have to be more deceitful and less open with American outfits than those in other countries.''

''I don't understand,'' James admitted.

''To put it bluntly,'' Manning began, ''the intelligence networks of the United States are not secure. We can't trust them because the Freedom of Information Act makes it possible for sensitive material to wind up on the front pages of major newspapers before it has even been declassified.''

''Journalists fond of sensationalism, politicians seeking publicity, even ex-CIA and FBI members themselves can reveal information that jeopardizes current covert operations,'' McCarter declared as he shook a cigarette from a pack of Players. ''Those bastards don't give a damn about national security. Get some press coverage and a spot on prime-time television. That's what matters to them.''

''The Constitution grants freedom of speech and freedom of the press,'' Calvin James commented.

''And that's necessary for a free society,'' Katz agreed. ''No one in this room finds any fault with that. The constitution also gives you the right to keep and bear arms, but that doesn't give you the right to blow your neighbor's head off because he plays his stereo too loudly. Rights and privileges also carry the burden of responsibility, something far too many people tend to forget.''

''I don't think we'd better work with the Feds or the local police this time,'' Manning advised. ''Whoever these Black Alchemists are, they've got a national organization. That means it's possible they also have connections with law enforcement. Perhaps on a federal level.''

"But this Jenson character is the only lead we've got," James began. "If we don't work with the cops and the FBI, how are we going to get any information out of the bum?"

"We'll just have to convince the police to let us borrow him for a while," Encizo said with a shrug.

"I don't think I want to hear this," Brognola groaned.

7

He called himself Cercueil. No one knew if this was his real name or a name adopted decades ago when he was head of François Duvalier's secret police in Haiti. Maurice Cercueil had been one of the most feared men in his native land. Cercueil—"Coffin"—suited him.

Cercueil sat at the head of the conference table. He was a great black shadow. His skin was as dark as ebony wood and he wore a formal black suit. Although indoors, he wore a pair of dark glasses and a silk top hat. Cercueil may have seemed ridiculous to anyone who did not understand the significance of his clothing. The Haitian secret police, called the Ton Ton Macout, wore dark glasses because they were named after the demons of the night who abduct children in voodoo folklore. The black top hat was reminiscent of Baron Samedi, the leader of the Legions of the Dead.

"Gentlemen," Cercueil began, speaking English for the sake of the American at the table. "We have a problem."

Colonel Pierre Guerre raised his scant eyebrows. Born Pierre de Gasget, he had formerly been a captain in the Haitian Army. After joining forces with Cercueil, he had changed his name to "Colonel War." A tall muscular man with a complexion the shade of black coffee, Guerre was the military strategist of the Black Alchemists.

He liked to wear uniforms. Since Guerre's arrival in the United States, he had bought a variety of American uniforms and military decorations from popular mail-order companies. He sat to Cercueil's right, dressed in a U.S. Marine blue dress uniform. His chest was decorated with an assortment of military campaign ribbons and insignia that included such odd combinations as a U.S. Army Good Conduct Medal beneath a replica of a Nazi S.S. emblem.

Despite his fetish, Guerre was a competent intelligence officer and strategist. He was also a cold-blooded killer. The ivory-gripped .45 automatic on his hip was not just another ornament.

"You're referring to the incident in Illinois?" Guerre asked.

"What happened in Illinois?" Farley Cole demanded, fumbling for a fresh pack of cigarettes.

Cole was the only American among the leaders of the Black Alchemists. In contrast to the flamboyant Haitians, he dressed in a sweat shirt and blue jeans. A thin sad-faced man, he wore his hair in a wild Afro that resembled a clump of black ferns.

Farley Cole had formerly been a professional chemist for a major corporation. Unfortunately his greed proved greater than his ethics, and he decided to process heroin for the Detroit syndicate. His role in the narcotic trade was discovered when several mobsters squealed to the District Attorney and agreed to turn state's evidence.

During Cole's six years in prison, he developed a persecution complex. He convinced himself that society had punished him and rewarded the gangster stool pigeons because he was black and they were white.

He never felt guilt or remorse for his actions. After all, the mob had seduced him. Thus Cole considered himself to be a victim of white oppression. The fact that most of the heroin was sold in black-ghetto sections in Detroit never bothered Cole. The honkies had used him and the honkies were going to pay.

"One of our people was caught putting cyanide in toothpaste," Cercueil explained, toying with a black swagger stick that featured a silver skull handle.

"Caught?" Cole gasped, choking on cigarette smoke. "You mean arrested?"

"Relax, Cole," Guerre urged. "Panic will only make matters worse. *Oui*."

"The goddamn cops will break that dumb bastard," Cole snapped. "Most of the people who are working for us are junkies and anarchist nitwits. How long do you think an idiot like that will keep his mouth shut?"

"Why don't you concentrate on your chemistry sets and leave these matters to us?" Guerre said in a cold hard voice.

"I'm supposed to have blind faith in your judgment?" Cole sneered. "Your toy-soldier act is a pain in the ass, Guerre. What great combat experience did you get while you were in the Haitian Army? Papa Doc didn't even let his military carry guns because he was afraid of a coup."

Guerre's face tensed with anger. It would be a pleasure to rearrange Cole's features with a .45 slug. Of course, they would dispose of the Yankee maggot when he was no longer needed. The thought helped Guerre control his temper.

"At least the Ton Ton Macout had some firsthand experience killing people," Cole continued, directing his verbal venom at Cercueil. "You were the head of Papa Doc's secret police—just as Himmler was for Hitler, right? But your goddamn Ton Ton Macout weren't exactly subtle. Carrying machine guns in plain view, raping peasant girls in broad daylight and shooting citizens for sport isn't exactly the sort of background that suggests your people are experts at clandestine operations, Cercueil."

"Let me kill him now," Guerre said, speaking to Cercueil in patois, a Haitian Creole dialect that Cole did not understand. "He has lost his nerve, Maurice."

"We did not hire him for his courage," Cercueil replied in the same tongue. "Be patient, *mon ami*."

"What are you talking about?" Cole demanded, suddenly aware that his rash remarks may have put his life in danger.

"We're wondering whether or not to allow you to attend these conferences in the future," Cercueil lied smoothly. "After all, you're only interested in the money, Cole. How reliable can you be? A man who would help blackmail his own government...."

"It's a white man's government," Cole spat. "Not mine."

"Spare us another lecture about how you suffered because of your skin color," the Black Alchemist leader said with a sigh. "The chemicals you prepare for us are used to sabotage goods which are purchased by Americans—black as well as white. Don't pretend to have any scruples, Cole."

"You don't have any business criticizing me," Cole snapped. He regretted the remark as soon as he made it. Cercueil was not a man to trifle with.

"I served President Duvalier loyally until his death in 1971," Cercueil declared proudly. "I would have served his son as well if Jean-Claude had not betrayed me. Colonel Guerre and I have a goal that justifies our role in the Black Alchemist operations. We intend to return to Haiti and seize control from that arrogant pup."

"So what are you going to do about that moron the cops caught in Illinois?" Cole asked. "Within forty-eight hours the pigs'll have him singing like a goddamn canary in heat."

"So let him talk." Guerre shrugged. "He doesn't know about us or where our headquarters are located."

"That's true," Cercueil agreed, tapping the death's-head handle of his cane against his palm. "But he might tell the authorities about the location of the Chicago base. If the police raid it, our operations throughout the Midwest would be in jeopardy."

"Then you want the man terminated?" Guerre asked.

"Within forty-eight hours," Cercueil confirmed.

8

"There's Jenson," Colonel Katzenelenbogen announced, gazing through an infrared Starlite night viewer. "He's shaved off his beard, but I recognize him from the mug shots."

Calvin James sat next to the Israeli behind the steering wheel of a Volvo parked half a block from the Springfield Police Department. In addition to the Starlite viewer, Katz also had a Hunter's Ear longrange listening device trained on the police station and the five men who had emerged from it.

Howard Jenson, clad in denim, his hands cuffed behind his back, was sandwiched between four men. The escorts wore "executive" uniforms—single-breasted suits, white shirts and striped ties. Katz had little doubt who they were.

"Looks like the FBI has already convinced the local police to put Jenson into its custody," the Israeli declared as he watched the group walk to a pair of sedans parked at the curb. Two more Feds waited by the cars.

"Thought that might happen," Katz muttered. "We'll have to put plan B into action."

"Jesus," James whispered. "I never figured I'd be helping kidnap a prisoner from the FBI."

James had been stunned by how rapidly events had unfolded within the last eight hours. After his initial briefing at Stony Man Headquarters, he had been taken to an enormous arms room containing an incredible assortment of firearms, explosives, knives and other weapons. His SWAT weapons had been left behind at the Hilldale Bank because the guns could be easily traced if they had to be discarded during the mission.

David McCarter had acted as tour guide through the arms room. The Briton told James that he could help himself to whatever weapons he desired. McCarter also urged him to keep his selection practical for the type of mission involved. The SAS veteran further advised James to pick reliable cartridge. "Make your decision, and remember: your life might depend on it later."

James chose weapons he had previous experience with, and refamiliarized himself with them at an indoor firing range. Then he was issued special combat clothing and other gear. Finally, he joined the other members of Phoenix Force to discuss strategy.

Plan A was conceived when Kurtzman's computer links discovered the FBI planned to take custody of Howard Jenson. Phoenix Force hoped to beat the Feds to the Springfield station. Then Manning and James would simply impersonate FBI agents and remove Jenson from police custody without any hassle.

Plan B would not be so easy.

"Well," Katz began as he picked up a communicator. "At least we won't have to use plan C."

"Yeah," James sighed with relief. Plan C would

have gone into effect if they were forced to break Jenson out of his jail cell.

"Let's not be too sure," said Katz, putting the transceiver back into its cradle. "Looks like the competition just showed up."

The Israeli quickly grabbed his Starlite viewer and locked in on the police station, where half a dozen strangers in jeans, dark jackets and ski masks had suddenly materialized. The assailants pointed an assortment of silencer-equipped weapons at the FBI agents and Howard Jenson. The startled Feds hastily shoved their prisoner to the pavement and reached for sidearms under their jackets.

Through the Hunter's Ear, Katz heard the muffled *phut-phut-phut* of silenced gunshots. Three FBI men tumbled to the sidewalk as the terrorists raked the group with gunfire. The remaining Feds jumped behind the closest sedan for cover.

The attackers moved in for the kill. Two FBI agents returned fire with their pistols. A terrorist crumpled to the pavement, clutching his bullet-torn abdomen. The others scrambled for the shelter of parked vehicles.

"Go!" Katz snapped into the transceiver.

James immediately shifted the Volvo into drive and stomped upon the gas pedal. The car squealed toward the gunfight. No one in Phoenix Force had foreseen that the Black Alchemists might try to rescue or terminate Jenson. The Phoenix Force team would have to use its limited arsenal and play it by ear.

In case it needed to take out the police or the Feds,

Phoenix Force had brought several Bio-Inoculator pistols and two Anschutz air rifles loaded with sleep darts. These nonlethal weapons are not suited for serious combat. James did not know how much deadly hardware his companions carried, but all he had was a .45-caliber Colt Combat Commander—hardly an even match against opponents armed with submachine guns.

"Shit, man," he rasped as the Volvo sped toward the terrorists.

"Watch out for the backup team," Katz warned, drawing an Israeli-made .357 Eagle autoloader from shoulder leather.

"Backup team?"

"Six terrorists wouldn't try to pull a stunt like this without a backup," Yakov explained. "Probably in a vehicle. Maybe several."

"Great," James groaned.

Two figures wearing ski masks appeared in front of the Volvo, aimed subguns at the car and opened fire. Bullets smashed into the windshield, instantly cracking it into a jagged road-map pattern.

James ducked as low as possible behind the wheel. He clenched his teeth and resisted the urge to swerve away from the gunmen. His foot remained solidly down on the gas pedal.

"Eat my fender," he snarled.

The terrorists cried out and tried to dodge the charging Volvo. One was not fast enough: the car slammed into him with terrific force. His body was hurled eight feet. It cartwheeled across the street to the curb. Broken and bleeding, the terrorist died as he had lived—in a gutter.

James savagely turned the steering wheel to the right. The Volvo veered sharply, lurched to the curb and jumped onto the sidewalk. The black warrior stomped on the brake and killed the engine, and he and Katz quickly tumbled out.

After witnessing the fate of their comrade, the surviving terrorists had again retreated to cover, and continued to fire at Katz and James. Luckily for Phoenix Force, the terrorists used their weapons with plenty of desperation but little skill.

A black Mazda suddenly shot into the middle of the street. Rafael Encizo drove while David McCarter poked the muzzle of his Ingram M-10 out the passenger-side window. The Briton fired on a trio of terrorists crouched behind a squad car on the curb. He hit two of them. The impact smashed them into the prowl car. They slumped lifeless to the ground. The third terrorist shrieked in horror but managed to escape the horizontal volley of metal hail.

Katz and James took advantage of the distraction. As James covered him, the Israeli spun from the shelter of the Volvo and dashed to an Oldsmobile that a terrorist was using for cover. James was surprised and impressed by the middle-aged Israeli's speed and agility.

The enemy gunman's attention was still on the Mazda as Katz scrambled to the rear of the Olds. The terrorist either sensed danger or caught a glimpse of movement. He turned sharply to see the Israeli's .357 autoloader pointed at him.

With a deranged snarl, the gunman swung his Smith & Wesson M-76 submachine gun at Katz. The Phoenix Force commander responded by rapidly triggering his Eagle pistol. Two 125-grain jacketed hollowpoint projectiles punched into the man's chest.

One of the potent man stoppers ripped through the terrorist, mushrooming through a lung before making a gory exit through his back. The other struck the center of his chest and burst the bone to send fragments into his heart. The gunman's body was thrown backward across the pavement, leaving a crimson trail.

Only one member of the terrorist hit team remained. Young Frank Tate squatted behind a squad car, face dripping sweat, knuckles white as he gripped the frame of his Skorpion machine pistol. Tate was a half-baked anarchist who claimed to be a Marxist although he had never read the *Communist Manifesto* and he thought Adolf Hitler had written *Das Kapital*. He also claimed to be an atheist, but now he found himself praying for deliverance.

The response to his supplications was immediate. A small object struck the side of his head as sharp pain lanced through his brain and hot lava seemed to bubble inside his skull. His last thoughts were two questions: Did God strike me dead for my sins? Will I go to hell? He died without knowing the answer to the former, but no doubt found out about the latter.

"Did we get them all?" Encizo spoke into his transceiver as he braked the Mazda.

"Everybody's down except our guys," replied Gary Manning, who had the best observation post.

"What about Jenson and the Feds?"

"Only one Fed survived," the Canadian replied.

"I shot him and Jenson with sleep darts. They're both napping. Nailed one of the terrorists too, but I don't think he'll ever wake up. Bastard moved his head just as I squeezed the trigger. Dart hit him right in the temple."

Blue-uniformed figures burst from the front door of the police station. The Springfield Police were not cowards. They were not stupid either. The cops had no intention of rushing into such a fierce firefight with just service revolvers. The officers who emerged from the building were decked out with flak jackets, riot helmets and shotguns.

"You can bet there are other cops at the windows with rifles and tear-gas canisters ready," James told Katz when he joined the Israeli.

"Show them your FBI ID," Yakov said. "Tell them we're a special antiterrorist strike force the Feds sent to back up their regular agents."

"Think they'll buy it?"

"They can see we're not wearing ski masks," Katz replied with a shrug.

"Heads up!" Manning's voice warned from the transceiver on Katz's belt.

A large van, the type used for moving furniture, suddenly appeared from the east. It rocketed toward the area like a mechanical behemoth and screeched to an abrupt halt. The back door rolled open and six men clad in terrorist chic—dark jackets and ski masks—hopped out.

"Wondered what happened to the backup team," Katz commented, almost casually.

Two terrorists dropped onto their bellies, instantly

setting up a belt-fed M-60 machine gun complete with bipod. The pair trained its formidable chatterbox on the police station and opened fire. A tidal wave of 7.62mm rounds lanced into the cops. Black-tipped armor-piercing projectiles punched through flak vests as if they were made of tissue paper. Bloodied bodies tumbled down the stairs as other police started shooting from the windows.

"*¡Cabrónes!*" Encizo growled with anger when he saw the slaughter.

The Cuban popped open the glove compartment and reached inside for a smooth-shelled M-26 hand grenade. Encizo bolted from the Mazda and dashed toward the machine gunners. Needles of pain traveled up his leg as the steel pin in his ankle made itself known. Ignoring his discomfort, the Cuban scrambled to a car parked a few yards from the M-60 team.

Crouched behind the vehicle, Encizo judged the approximate distance to the terrorists and pulled the pin from his M-26. Waiting for two heartbeats, he snapped the grenade at the machine gunners. It struck the ground, bounced and rolled to the killers before the detonator erupted.

The fragmentation grenade showed no mercy to man or machine. The blast sent the M-60 into the night sky, a mangled chunk of twisted steel. Ragged, torn fragments of human beings showered the street with grisly debris.

Three terrorists retreated behind the van. Unfortunately for them, their backs were turned to the camera shop on the roof of which Gary Manning watched them through the sights of a .41 Magnum Smith & Wesson revolver.

The Canadian aimed carefully, squeezed the trigger. The big S&W bucked and roared. A high-velocity .41 Magnum wadcutter crashed through a terrorist's skull. His head exploded like cabbage hit by a sledgehammer.

The ghastly corpse fell upon the remaining terrorists. The startled pair knew not the source of the new threat until Manning fired his Magnum again. Another .41-caliber devastator blasted into the chest of an enemy buttonman. The big projectile dropped through the terrorist's torso and made a gory exit between his shoulders.

"On the roof, shithead!" the burly driver of the van shouted as he emerged from the cab with a 12-gauge pump shotgun in his fist.

Although the driver had seen Manning, he failed to notice Keio Ohara. The Japanese warrior had climbed down a fire escape to the alley and was stealthily creeping toward the van, waiting for an opportunity to strike.

It arrived.

Ohara burst from the alley with a running leap. His right leg extended, he executed a *tobi-geri*, flying kick. His boot struck the door of the cab, slamming it upon the van driver. The shotgun clattered to the sidewalk.

The other terrorist pivoted sharply, a compact M-11 Ingram in his fists. He fired a rapid salvo at Ohara. Half a dozen copper-jacketed .380 rounds pierced flesh and pulverized human organs.

The driver's body slumped to the pavement, his chest a crimson pulp. His comrade with the M-11 had blasted the wrong target. Keio Ohara had dived to the sidewalk in a fast *mae-ukemi*, shoulder roll. None of the .380 slugs had touched his body as he tumbled across the cement.

The roll carried Ohara to the terrorist gunman. Before the startled killer could re-aim his Ingram, Ohara struck once more. From a prone position, the Phoenix Force pro lashed out a long leg and kicked the M-11 from his opponent's grasp.

He immediately followed through with a vicious scissors kick, his legs trapping the gunman's ankles in a firm vise. A hard twist sent the terrorist facefirst to the sidewalk. Ohara pounced on his back and lashed the side of his hand across the base of his skull. The *shuto* stroke cracked bone, severed the spinal cord and smashed the man's face into concrete.

Only one terrorist had survived the firefight. Terrified, the man panicked and ran into the street. McCarter cut off his escape route and fired a 3-round burst at his feet, hoping to urge him to surrender.

The gunman bolted in terror toward the squad cars. This put him directly in the line of fire of the police riflemen whose bullets plastered him against a cop car. He slid to the sidewalk and bowed his shattered head against a tire.

"Well, that's the last of them," Manning's voice announced with relief.

"Are you certain?" Katz asked via his communicator.

"Yeah. None of the bad guys made it, unless you count Jenson. Keio tried to take one of them alive, but things didn't work out that way."

"Let's grab Jenson and pull out," Katz said.

"Gary, get down here in case we have to talk to the police."

"Right," Manning agreed.

"I sure hope Jenson is worth all this trouble," Calvin James remarked to Katz.

The Israeli replied, "We'll find out soon enough."

9

Howard Jenson groaned as he regained consciousness. Slowly he opened his eyes: the lids felt as if they were lined with lead. Fog seemed to surround him, but a brilliant globe of light burned through the mist.

"Your vision will clear in a minute or two," Calvin James told him. "You'll probably have some vertigo, so don't try to get up."

"Where am I?" Jenson asked. His jaw was numb, his speech slurred.

"You're still alive," Katzenelenbogen declared. "That ought to be enough for now."

The fog lifted, but the glare of a 150-watt bulb from a gooseneck lamp nearly blinded him. Jenson squinted and turned away.

"Who are you guys? You're not cops, are you?"

"We're not Black Alchemists either," Yakov told him bluntly. "Your comrades tried to kill you tonight."

"Bullshit," Jenson replied, unable to see his captors clearly. "They shot down those federal bastards to try to rescue me."

"Shee-it," James snorted, slipping into ghetto jive because he knew Jenson was a product of the streets. "Those dudes used machine guns like they were spraying for roaches, and you would have been just another bug, man.''

"Screw you, nigger," Jenson growled.

"Watch your mouth," Rafael Encizo warned. "Unless you want it washed out with Janitor-In-A-Drum."

"No sweat." James chuckled. "I don't give a damn what a two-bit junkie punk calls me. He's not worth getting excited about."

"He's not worth anything period unless he tells us about the Black Alchemists," Katz remarked dryly.

Katz thrust his prosthetic limb under the lamp. Jenson gasped fearfully when he saw the steel hooks snap together like a bear trap.

"We don't have all night," the Israeli said in an icy voice. "If you insist on wasting our time, I may become impatient and decide to snip off a finger for every rude remark that slithers out of that cesspool you use for a mouth. Understood?"

Jenson bobbed his head in reply.

"Look, sonny," James began. "We know all about you. You're an ex-con with a heroin monkey on your back. If the Feds locked you up and kept you cold turkey for a few days, you'd blab your head off to get a fix. You're a waste product, man. Your buddies know they can't rely on you to keep your mouth shut. It would be easier to dust you than try to break you out of the joint."

"You guys don't scare me," Jenson said, but the tremble in his voice betrayed him.

"We don't intend to," Katz told him. "You've got a choice, Jenson. You talk to us now or we hand you over to the FBI. The Feds will simply wait for heroin withdrawal to break you down. Then you'll stand trial for conspiracy to commit murder, attempted murder and whatever else they can throw at you. If your comrades get to you, either before you go to prison or while you're locked up, you know what they'll do to you.''

''And what can you offer that's any better?'' Jenson asked.

''Tell us everything you know about the Black Alchemists, and we'll see to it your cooperation goes on record to the Feds,'' James told him.

''Big deal,'' Jenson growled.

''It will be a big deal if you can help us save lives,'' Encizo snapped.

''We could tell you we'd let you go or set you up with a new identity in the Virgin Islands,'' Katz added. ''But even you aren't stupid enough to believe that.''

''How do I know you won't just kill me?''

''Our word is good,'' Katz replied. ''But I'm certain a man who would put cyanide in toothpaste doesn't understand what honor means.''

''Jenson,'' said Calvin James, removing a leather packet from his jacket. ''Do you know what scopolamine is?''

''Huh?''

''Scopolamine is the most potent truth serum in the world,'' James explained, unzipping the pouch to remove a hypodermic syringe. ''If I give you this injection, you'll answer any question we ask. The only problem with scopolamine is it causes the heartbeat to accelerate. It could kill you. That's why we don't want to use it. But we'll have no choice if you refuse to talk.''

"You're bluffing," Jenson said, attempting to disguise the fear in his voice.

"Okay, fellas." James shrugged. "Dumb ass wants it the hard way."

"Should we hold him down?" Encizo asked.

"Yeah," James answered. "And get my stethoscope and sphygmomanometer. That's the device used for taking blood pressure. Only way we'll be able to judge the effects of the scopolamine."

"Jesus Christ! I'll talk, dammit!"

"Very well," Katz said, placing a tape recorder on the coffee table, within the circle of light. "When I turn on the machine, give us your confession and all the details. Start by saying you're doing this voluntarily. We don't want evidence kicked out of court on a technicality."

"Turn it on."

Katz pressed the start button and Jenson leaned forward to speak into the microphone.

"My name is Howard Jenson. I make this statement of my own free will. I have not been threatened or bribed in any way. Nor have I been denied sleep, food or drink, or subjected to any unreasonable stress."

The three members of Phoenix Force were surprised by Jenson's preamble. James showed Jenson a hand. The thumb and forefinger formed a circle to indicate that the captive was doing okay. He'd obviously had practice at this.

James, Katz and Encizo were silent during Jenson's confession, unwilling to leave voice prints on the tape that might lead to their identification. They listened quietly to Jenson as he recalled how he had been drafted into a conspiracy.

Jenson knew nothing of the Black Alchemists. His heroin supplier in Chicago, a black pusher known only as Joystick, had offered him six ounces of white powder as an advance payment for sabotaging the toothpaste at the Blue Label Corporation.

Jenson was given forged ID, $3,000, and enough horse to support his habit for two weeks as initial payment. Then he applied for employment at the Blue Label Corporation. There were four jobs available on the assembly line.

Although the promise of heroin was more than enough to buy Jenson's cooperation, he became curious about the reason for his covert mission. Why did Joystick want him to do this? The dealer was obviously working for someone else.

Jenson began to follow Joystick's activities. He surreptitiously shadowed the pusher every night for nine days. On three occasions, Joystick met with a group of hardcases at a warehouse in the North Shore district. The dope dealer treated the tough guys with considerable respect, not the way he behaved among a group of his junkie customers.

The big boys consisted of blacks, whites and Hispanics, but the leader was a muscle-bound black guy with a shaved head who always wore dark glasses and a short-sleeved blue shirt. Jenson later learned this mystery man was a Haitian refugee who called himself Tigershark.

Word on the street claimed Tigershark had a lot of money and plenty of torpedoes to protect it. Apparently the Haitian had contacts with other drug dealers besides Joystick. He also met with members of certain Hispanic street gangs, black militant groups and assorted anarchists from a variety of ethnic origins.

Unfortunately Jenson could not confirm any of these rumors. Joystick, realizing he was being tailed, sent a trio of junkie hoods to teach Jenson a painful lesson. They gave him a mild beating that left him bruised but not broken.

"This is just a warning, man," a wild-eyed thug told him. "You keep your nose outta Joystick's business or next time we'll cut your ass like a Christmas turkey."

Jenson heeded this advice. He followed orders and put the chemicals in the toothpaste. He claimed he did not know it was poison. A watchful supervisor caught him as he attempted to carry out the sabotage that led to his arrest.

Katzenelenbogen switched off the tape recorder. "What's the address of this warehouse?"

Jenson told him.

"Good boy," James remarked as he pressed the plunger of the syringe to squirt some liquid from the needle. "You want to give yourself this shot or do I have to do it?"

Jenson glared at his captors. "You said I wouldn't have to take that truth-serum shit if I cooperated."

"This isn't scopolamine," James explained. "It's ninety-five millimeters of thorazine. Same stuff that was in the sleep dart. You're just going to take another nap for a while."

"Why drug me again?"

"The hell with this bastard," Encizo growled. "I've got a B-I pistol. Let me shoot another sleep dart into the son of a bitch."

"Give me the damn needle," Jenson said hastily.

"Just pretend it's a fix, Howie."

Jenson injected the drug into his arm. In less than a minute, he was unconscious. James took his pulse, checked his heartbeat, peeled back an eyelid.

"He's out," the black man declared. "But we'd better leave somebody with him in case he wakes up before we can wrap things up at the warehouse."

"Rafael," Katz turned to the Cuban. "You're elected."

"My ankle hasn't slowed me down yet, Yakov," Encizo replied glumly.

"I saw you limping after the firefight," the Israeli told him. "You're staying with Jenson. The little bastard may have lied to us. We may have to use the scopolamine yet."

"I don't think he lied," Calvin James commented.

"We'd better be ready for trouble anyway," the Israeli replied.

James switched off the 150-watt bulb that had blinded their prisoner. "Man," he remarked. "You guys sure know how to have one hell of a wild night on the town."

10

"I thought you knew Chicago," David McCarter complained to Calvin James.

"I was born on the south side," James replied as he drove the Volvo past the Dyche Stadium exit. "Never spent much time in the North Shore area. Besides, I haven't been back here for a while."

"Try to excuse David," Katzenelenbogen apologized. "He tends to get a bit impatient when he knows a battle is looming."

The Israeli sat in the back seat, gazing at the Sears Tower, which rose majestically above dozens of smaller buildings. The Chicago skyline contains three of the tallest buildings on earth: the Sears Tower, the John Hancock Center and the Standard Oil Building. The Israeli was impressed.

"You enjoy combat?" James asked the British warrior.

"I enjoy being alive," McCarter replied. "And a man never feels more alive than in combat."

"It's also a good way to get yourself killed."

"The best," McCarter agreed cheerfully. "Look, mate. None of us are in this for money or glory. Oh, we get a bit of extra pocket cash, but hardly enough to make it worth the risks. Glory? No parades for us.

Top secret, hush-hush, for your eyes only and all that rot. Nobody knows what we're doing.''

"I'm on this mission to help stop a bunch of killers,'' James declared.

"Naturally,'' the Briton nodded. "But why were you chosen for the job? One of the main reasons is because you're good in combat. A man is seldom good at something he doesn't enjoy.''

"Somebody has to do it,'' James insisted, aware how corny the expression sounded.

"And luckily we qualify. Come now, Calvin. We're all dedicated to fighting terrorism and protecting the interests of the free world. We all believe in what we're doing, but if we didn't love the excitement and adventure, we wouldn't be here.''

"How long do you think it'll be before you stop a bullet?'' James asked dryly.

"Already did.'' McCarter shrugged. "Happened a couple times, but so far no bullets have stopped *me*.''

"As a man who likes to think of himself as relatively sane,'' Katz interjected, "I hate to agree with McCarter, but as an old war-horse myself, I understand him. We fight for a good cause, true, but we fear retirement more than the battlefield. We'd all prefer a quick death in combat to winding up in a nursing home as ancient senile relics who have a thrilling afternoon by playing checkers in the dayroom.''

"Maybe you've got a point at that,'' James was forced to admit.

"Foxhound One, this is Foxhound Two,'' Gary Manning's voice crackled from Katz's radio.

Manning and Keio Ohara followed the Volvo in a Mazda rental. Manning had once spent three months in Chicago while on assignment for North America International, supervising security procedures. Thus, he had volunteered to drive the second vehicle.

"According to the map we should be getting close now," he declared. "After we pass the Baha'i Temple, watch for Wilmette Street. Connor Drive is a side street from there."

"All right," Katz replied. "We'll run a quiet recon past the warehouse and meet about two blocks farther on. Just cruise past the place. We don't want to get anyone suspicious."

"Affirmative," the voice of Gary Manning responded from the speaker in its usual businesslike tone.

Two minutes later, James located Connor Drive. He drove the Volvo along a column of warehouses. Number thirty-four was where Jenson claimed the mysterious Tigershark had set up his headquarters.

A long gold Cadillac was parked in front. Its doors opened and three black men emerged. Two resembled pro football players dressed in street clothes. The third looked like a Hollywood stereotype of a ghetto pimp. He wore a white suit with a wide-brimmed hat and a bright scarlet cape.

James clucked his tongue with disgust as he drove past. "That must be Joystick. Goddamn predator. His type hustles black girls on the street and sells dope to black kids and then brags about how they're getting over on whitey. Christ, I hate them."

"Because of your sister?" McCarter inquired.

James removed his eyes from the road long enough to glare at the Briton. "Leave her out of this."

"Can you?" Katz asked flatly. "We know your sister died from a heroin overdose."

"Susie was just a kid. A junior in high school. The class pusher got her started on pills. Usual stuff. Susie graduated to cocaine and couldn't afford the habit. A maggot known as Sweet Leroy loaned her a couple hundred dollars to cover expenses. Then she owed him a favor. Before long he had her turning tricks as one of his hookers. Sweet Leroy believed in keeping his girls under control by getting them hooked on heroin. I still think she wanted out and he killed her."

"You wouldn't be thinking of settling any old scores with Leroy, would you?" Katz asked.

"The son of a bitch is still in prison. As long as he stays there, he's safe."

"Nobody can blame you for having a grudge against pimps and dope dealers," said McCarter. "But we can't have it get in the way of the mission."

"It won't."

"And no stunts like that one you pulled in San Francisco a couple years ago," the Israeli warned.

"What stunt?"

"I believe Katz is talking about the time you took a switchblade away from a pimp," McCarter said, "and then stuck it up his arse."

"That was an accident," James replied, unable to suppress a smile. "He sort of sat on it."

"No more accidents," Katz said sternly. "Understood?"

"Don't worry."

"Pull over to the curb," the Israeli instructed. "We'll wait for Gary and Keio and then decide how to handle the warehouse."

TWO MUSCULAR HOODS were stationed in front of the warehouse when the Volvo slowly approached. The pair stiffened when the car slowed to a halt. One of the thugs reached inside his Levi jacket, but the other man whispered something to him, probably a warning not to draw his weapon—yet.

"Hi, guys," Calvin James announced casually as he opened the Volvo door. "Man, am I glad to see you dudes."

"You want somethin', fella?" growled a sentry who resembled a fireplug with clothes on.

"We're lost," James told him, stepping from the car with a road map in his hand. "You know how to get to Joliet from here? You know, where they've got the Illinois State Prison?"

"What the...?"

David McCarter poked the barrel of his Bio-Inoculator through an open window and squeezed the trigger. The human fireplug groaned discreetly and slapped a palm to his neck. He touched the feathered end of a hypodart lodged in his flesh.

His eyes rolled upward, his legs buckled. He fell to his knees, dazed by the thorazine. The other hood desperately reached for a gun in his belt. McCarter fired another B-I pistol. The goon cried out when a dart struck his chest.

The muscle boy pulled a Charter Arms .38 revolver from his belt. James lunged forward. His right leg executed a lightning-quick *tae-kwondo* kick. The edge of his foot struck the guy's wrist, snapping the radius and ulna on contact. The gun fell to the ground.

James slashed a side-of-the-hand stroke to the man's mouth. Blood burst from the hoodlum's upper lip as he fell against the warehouse wall. James rammed an elbow into his opponent's breastbone. The sentry gasped and slumped into a heap.

McCarter emerged from the Volvo, Ingram machine pistol in hand. He calmly approached the first sentry who was on his knees, dazed, clutching his neck. The Briton kicked him in the face.

James and McCarter quickly bound the thugs' wrists and ankles with unbreakable plastic cuffs. Katz joined them with his Uzi in one hand and an M-16 in the other. He handed the assault rifle to James. Then they waited for Gary Manning and Keio Ohara to signal that they were in position to start the raid.

THE CANADIAN AND JAPANESE MEMBERS of Phoenix Force, who had approached the rear of the building on foot, found a single sentry armed with a pump shotgun at the back door. Manning fired a hypodart into the side of his neck. Thorazine raced into his jugular and he crumpled to the ground.

Manning lowered his Anschutz air rifle and grunted with satisfaction. Then he put down the air gun and gathered up the nasty H&K MP-5. Ohara stood beside him with a .45-caliber M-10 Ingram.

The pair closed in, two silent shadows in the night. When they reached the door, Manning unslung a black ditty bag from his shoulder and removed a block of gray putty. It was his favorite old British plastic, CV-38; a low-velocity explosive good for rending and tearing. Manning only used the compound when he needed a low-boom explosive.

Ohara bound the unconscious guard and dragged him to shelter in another warehouse. Manning knelt by the door and prepared to fit the explosive putty into the frame.

A shadow suddenly blocked the moonlight. Manning turned to see the silhouette of a man's head and shoulders. The shape wielded a claw hammer in its fist, aimed at the Canadian's head.

Manning ducked. The tool missed his skull by inches. His guts knotted as he felt the rush of air against his left ear.

When his assailant's forearm struck Manning's shoulder, the Canadian quickly trapped the limb with his left hand, pinning it to his deltoid. Before his attacker could respond, Manning drove a right uppercut between the man's splayed legs.

With a half moan, half gasp, the attacker wilted to the ground, uttering a choked gurgle of agony. Manning shut him up by delivering a solid punch to the point of his chin.

Quickly setting the explosive in place, Manning inserted a pencil detonator and set the dial for fifteen seconds. Then he carried the unconscious guard to safety behind the next building. Ohara raised his eyebrows with surprise when he saw Manning's burden.

"Cuff this guy, Keio." The Canadian dumped the

sentry to the ground. "Make it quick. Show time starts—"

The explosion cut off his words. Under the circumstances, there was no need for him to finish the sentence.

11

The explosion served two functions. First: it was a signal for Katz, McCarter and James. Second: it was one hell of a distraction for the men inside the warehouse. The hoodlums were still gaping at the remnants of the back door when Calvin James kicked in the front.

The black hardcase charged into the building, M-16 held ready for trouble. David McCarter dived in right behind him. They plunged into a storage section filled with wooden crates and startled thugs who scrambled in all directions. James's sharp eye caught a glimpse of Joystick as the flamboyant dope dealer dashed for shelter behind a column of cargo boxes.

James hoped Joystick would stay alive long enough for him to personally take care of the pusher. However, Joystick did not present an immediate threat. Several enemy gunmen did.

A pimple-faced youth with a stringy blond beard grabbed a CAR-15 automatic carbine from a corner. Joystick's two black bodyguards pulled snub-nose Magnums from shoulder leather. Two Hispanic thugs made a desperate dive for a card table where they had left their pistols.

Dropping to one knee, James opened fire with the

M-16 on full auto. Four 5.56mm slugs ripped into the bearded goon's chest. The impact sent the hood flying into a stack of cardboard containers. He knocked the boxes across the room as his corpse fell.

A .357 round cracked through the air just above James's head. Had the black Phoenix Force recruit not been kneeling, the bullet would have killed him. Calvin James was too busy to realize how close he had come to death.

He continued to blast the enemy gunmen. Three M-16 projectiles smashed into the throat and face of Joystick's closest triggerman. The bodyguard's lower jaw exploded, spewing blood, teeth and bone splinters. A bullet pierced the guy's windpipe and shattered vertebrae.

Before the first bodyguard's corpse hit the floor, James fired a volley of 5.56mm messengers into the upper torso of the brute's partner. The pusher's pet goon suffered an abrupt cardiac arrest caused by two bullets through the heart. The second bodyguard crashed into a water cooler and slid lifeless to the floor.

David McCarter had hit the floor in a fast shoulder roll that carried him to the shelter of a large metal chest. The Briton's battle-honed instincts seemed to guide him into a cover area like a homing pigeon. Combat was McCarter's element, like an eagle stalking prey from the sky.

The two Hispanic hoods managed to grab their weapons on the card table, but they did not live long enough to fire a single shot. McCarter sprayed the pair with lethal Ingram fire. Blood and brains splashed the nearest wall. The card table collapsed when the two corpses fell upon it.

A black man wearing a blue shirt and sunglasses appeared on a catwalk overlooking the storage room. He thrust an M-76 S&W submachine gun in McCarter's direction. Katzenelenbogen, stationed at the doorway, spotted the gunman and instantly raised his Uzi subgun.

The Israeli's weapon hammered out a rapid 3-round burst. Hot 9mm rounds burned through flesh. The killer fell forward into a plywood handrail. It refused to support his weight and broke. The man shrieked as he plunged twelve feet to the concrete below.

A large barrel-chested black man, also clad in a blue shirt, poked a .45-caliber Star PD pistol around the edge of a stack of crates and fired hastily at Katz. The battle-wise Israeli had already ducked behind the doorframe. The big 230-grain bullet splintered wood, but failed to strike flesh.

McCarter's M-10 spat a trio of rounds at the pistolman. The slugs chewed fragments from the crates that protected the hoodlum, but failed to find their target. The startled man quickly retreated from his position. But not before McCarter got a good look at his face. The black man was bald and wore a pair of dark glasses on the bridge of his nose.

The Briton recalled Jenson's description of Tigershark, the Haitian who appeared to be the leader of the terrorist network in Illinois. Most of the hoods in the warehouse were probably local street trash and junkies. Tigershark was the most likely member to know about the Black Alchemist high command.

"Don't catch a bullet, you bastard," McCarter rasped. "You're worth more to us alive."

CALVIN JAMES HAD FAILED to notice Tigershark. He still wanted Joystick. James saw the crown of the pusher's white hat moving above a column of crates. Joystick was trying to work his way to the back exit.

Determined not to let him escape, James broke cover and dashed after the fleeing figure. He immediately regretted his rash decision. A hailstorm of enemy bullets sizzled all around.

A stray slug struck the forestock of the M-16. Black fiberglass burst apart and the projectile rang against the steel barrel beneath. The rifle was torn from James's hands. The SWAT-trained warrior quickly dived to the floor and rolled to the shelter of the crates, his hands numb from the shock of the bullet's impact.

Another black killer, dressed in a blue shirt and dark glasses, tried to cut down Calvin James. Armed with a Skorpion machine pistol, the gunman scrambled to a new position and tried to aim the Czech-made chatterbox at the elusive ex-cop.

The roar of Keio Ohara's Ingram abruptly terminated the terrorist's plan. Three .45 rounds knifed through flesh and muscle between the man's shoulder blades. His spinal cord and thoracic vertebrae were instantly destroyed. He was pitched forward and landed facefirst on the floor. The right lens of his dark glasses crunched on impact, sending shards into his eyes. But he was already dead.

Ohara and Gary Manning had entered through the

rear door while the enemy battled with the other members of Phoenix Force. Once again the unprepared terrorists were caught off guard by a surprise attack from an unexpected position. Two gunmen whirled to confront the new threat only to catch a tidal wave of 9mm slugs from Manning's H&K submachine gun.

The Canadian prepared to step over his slain opponents when he saw Tigershark dart into another room. Aware of the Haitian's potential as a source of information, Manning sprinted after him.

A white-trash Chicago hood with curly red hair and a Winchester carbine spotted the Canadian. He raised the buttstock to a shoulder and aimed at Manning's back. Keio Ohara's Ingram snarled and the top of the redhead's skull erupted like Mount Saint Helen when two .45 slugs slammed into his forehead.

Manning reached the door through which Tigershark had fled. Through a window in the door he saw the Haitian dump a pile of file folders into a metal trash can. Tigershark struck a match and dropped it in.

"Bastard's destroying his records," Manning growled as he raised a boot.

The Canadian smashed his foot into the door, breaking the lock. He lunged into the room, MP-5 pointed at the Haitian. Tigershark looked up sharply and automatically reached for the .45 Star in his belt. He changed his mind when he stared into the muzzle of Manning's machine pistol.

"Drop the gun," Manning ordered.

"As you wish, white man," Tigershark replied,

slowly easing the pistol from his belt. He dropped it to the floor and kicked it toward Manning.

"Move to the wall," the Canadian instructed. "Spread-eagle. No tricks."

Tigershark obediently moved to the wall and placed his palms flat on the surface. Manning failed to notice the Haitian's right hand was positioned next to a window, his fingers only a few inches from the wooden haft of a long-bladed machete on the sill.

Manning kept his H&K trained on the Haitian as he entered the office. The Canadian placed a foot on the trash can, tipped it over and quickly stomped the flames with his boots.

Suddenly Tigershark whirled from the wall, the machete in his fist. Steel struck steel as the thick blade knocked the H&K from Manning's grasp. With a bestial roar, Tigershark swung the jungle knife in a cross-body stroke.

Manning ducked under the murderous blade and avoided decapitation. The Haitian swung the big knife again. The Canadian dodged again and lashed a foot into Tigershark's gut.

The Haitian doubled over in pain, executing a backhand sweep with the machete as he did so. Manning rapidly stepped forward and chopped the sides of both hands into Tigershark's forearm. The twin *shuto* stroke jarred the ulnar nerve. The machete fell from numb fingers.

Tigershark was tough. He suddenly swung his left fist into Manning's jaw. The Canadian staggered backward two steps. Tigershark rammed a solid uppercut to his stomach. Manning's hands rose quickly.

He clapped the palms against his opponent's ears. Tigershark howled from the pain of at least one ruptured eardrum. Manning immediately punched him in the mouth as hard as he could.

The Haitian fell onto the desk. Manning seized him from behind and pumped a fist into his right kidney. Then he wrapped an arm around the terrorist's throat and pressed a palm against the side of his head.

Manning intended to choke the man just enough to render him unconscious. Tigershark refused to oblige. The Haitian reached overhead and clawed fingers at Manning's eyes. The Canadian sharply turned his face from the gouging attack. He increased pressure with the choke hold and pulled his adversary against the desk.

Tigershark's feet slipped. His body swung sharply to the left, but Manning held his head stationary. Vertebrae crunched as Tigershark's neck was broken. Manning released the Haitian and allowed Tigershark's corpse to limply fall to the floor.

"Aw, shit," Manning muttered with disgust.

JOYSTICK'S EFFORT TO ESCAPE proved to be in vain. He had fled behind the crates only to find himself boxed into a corner. The dope dealer's face was coated with sweat. Damp patches stained the white suit under both arms.

Trapped, he clenched his fist around a pearl-handled .22 Derringer. The pretty little handgun was fine for impressing street hookers and dumb junkies, but it was hardly a combat weapon. The dudes who hit the warehouse were packing goddamn machine guns. What good was a derringer against that kind of firepower?

Calvin James appeared behind a column of boxes. Joystick panicked and fired his diminutive weapon without aiming. James ducked behind the last crate. He heard the whine of metal against concrete when the .22 round ricocheted off the floor.

James returned fire with his Colt Commander. A big .45 slug chipped the wall above Joystick's head. The pusher dropped to the floor in a trembling heap.

"Don't waste my ass!" he cried, tossing the derringer. "I give, man! I give!"

"Hands on your head, maggot breath," James ordered as he cautiously advanced, Colt pistol held ready.

"Sure, bro," Joystick replied.

"Don't give me any of that 'brother' jive," James told him. "It's an insult from a jerk like you."

"Look," Joystick said, trembling, "I don't know what's comin' down, but I'll deal. Tell the Man. I'll deal."

"Yeah," James muttered. "Dealing is how you got into this in the first place."

He glanced down at the derringer and contemptuously kicked it across the floor.

"Where'd you find that thing? In a box of Crackerjacks?"

"Cut me a break, man," the pusher urged. "I'll make it worth your while."

"Keep talkin', cesspool mouth. You've just about convinced me to kill you."

Suddenly a bloodied form crashed into the crates, propelled by a burst of 9mm rounds from Katzenelenbogen's Uzi. Two boxes toppled from the stack and fell on James. The corner of a crate struck his wrist and knocked the .45 from his hand.

Calvin James fell into the wall, stunned by the unexpected blow. Joystick took advantage of the distraction. He scrambled to his feet and pulled an object from a hip pocket.

"Let's see what you had for breakfast, nigger," the pusher said, smiling.

He pressed the button of his switchblade and a six-inch blade snapped into view. Light danced along the sharp steel as Joystick advanced.

12

"Oh, shit," James rasped.

Joystick may not have known any more about guns than which end to hold. He was clearly more familiar with knives. The pusher assumed a fighting stance, holding the switchblade low in an underhand grip.

James recognized Joystick's expertise. The dealer was a product of the streets. He knew how to handle a blade. James backed away. Joystick smiled as he quickly shuffled forward. The switchblade suddenly struck like a metal cobra. Steel flashed near James's face.

The ex-SWAT sergeant recoiled from the blade. His left hand streaked inside his jacket. Joystick made another quick feint and lunged his knife at James's midsection.

Sharp steel struck. Cloth ripped and skin split under the razor edge. Joystick cried out in surprise and pain. Blood bubbled from a severed artery and spread quickly over the sleeve of his white suit.

Calvin James had drawn a G-96 "Boot 'n Belt" knife from a sheath attached to his Jackass Leather rig under his right arm. He had caught the pusher off guard with a rapid sideway slash of the five-inch blade.

Joystick jumped back. He stared at the G-96 dagger in James's left fist.

"Son of a bitch," the dealer hissed through clenched teeth.

He moved the switchblade to his left hand and tried to execute a quick stab from an unexpected direction. The trick may have worked if Joystick had been pitted against an inexperienced knife fighter. But Calvin James was a veteran of Chicago's south side.

James dodged the knife and deftly swung the heel of his right palm into the pusher's forearm. The switchblade was deflected toward the floor. James's left arm plunged forward.

The double-edged blade of the G-96 pierced Joystick's right side. It slipped between the ribs at the seventh intercostal space to stab into the pusher's liver. Joystick screamed as James slit him open and yanked the dagger from the terrible wound.

Joystick sunk to his knees. The switchblade fell from his grasp. He groaned in agony and clutched both hands to his ripped torso. James ended his agony by hammering the steel butt of his knife into the top of Joystick's head. The blow cracked the dope dealer's skull, and he fell on his face—dead.

Colonel Katz appeared at the edge of the row of crates. "You feel better now?"

"Better than I'd feel if this bastard had cut me instead," James admitted, wiping the G-96 blade on the slain pusher's white jacket.

"You said you could control your emotions," the Israeli commented.

"I said they wouldn't get in the way of our mission."

"You nearly got yourself killed when you chased after Joystick," Katz declared. "You have no right to risk one-fifth of our strike force because of a personal grudge. That was stupid and careless. If you had been wounded, we would have had to expose ourselves to danger in order to help you. Your life wasn't the only one your rash actions put at stake."

"I guess that didn't occur to me," James confessed. "I just didn't want Joystick to get away."

"None of them could have escaped," said Katz. "We had both exits covered and none of the windows are large enough for a man to climb through. We're professionals, James. We try not to leave anything to chance, and we try to avoid mistakes that could endanger the lives of our teammates."

"I'm sorry, Colonel."

Katz shrugged. "Well, this is the first time you've worked with Phoenix Force. On-the-job training is a bit rough, and God knows we've all made mistakes in the past. Actually you've done very well. Handled yourself in that firefight like a pro. You have plenty of skill and even more courage."

"Thank you, Colonel," James replied, warming to praise from the senior member of Phoenix Force.

"Call me Yakov or Katz," the Israeli told him. "Calling me colonel makes me feel as old as I am."

"None of our blokes got so much as a scratch," McCarter announced smugly as he joined the pair. "The only terrorists who survived are the sentries we took out before we crashed this party."

"Too bad." Katz frowned. "I'd hoped we'd get our hands on their commander for questioning."

"Well," said the Briton, taking a pack of Players from his pocket, "Gary caught up with that bald chap and tried to capture him, but you know how uncooperative terrorists can be. Bastard tried to burn his files. Gary saved what he could."

"I take it there isn't much left," Katz remarked.

"Most of the records are destroyed," McCarter answered, firing a cigarette. "Looks like Tigershark poured lighter fluid over them before setting them on fire."

"We'll just have to take what's left and hope we can find something worthwhile among the ashes," said the Israeli. "Let's pull out before the police decide to investigate tonight's fireworks display."

THEY DROVE TO A SMALL MOTEL located at the town limits of Marston, where Rafael was waiting and Howard Jenson, the captive, was still napping from the thorazine injection. After briefing the Cuban about the results of the raid, Phoenix Force examined the remains of the confiscated files.

The material was in French, a language understood by four members of Phoenix Force. Although charred and fragmented, the files still contained considerable information about several chemical sabotage schemes in Illinois.

One of the most welcome bits of information was a list of names of individuals who had put ground glass in cold cream. The people responsible for mutilating Mrs. Simms would not go unpunished. The most important data in the records was the remnants of several orders from a command center called Cancer Ward.

"Well, we've got a bunch of little fish for sure," Gary Manning remarked. "Are we going to squeeze them all for information?"

"That would take time, which is something we can't afford to waste," Katz replied. "Not with more and more sabotaged goods on the market. We'll turn everything over to Brognola, including Jenson, and let the Feds handle it."

"Great," Encizo muttered. "So we just go home?"

"Too bad we don't have any clues about the location of Cancer Ward," James commented as he checked Jenson's heartbeat and blood pressure.

"Maybe we do," McCarter declared, examining a charred piece of paper.

"What have you got, David?" Keio Ohara asked eagerly.

"A message from Cancer Ward instructing Tigershark to warn his men not to buy any cigarettes manufactured by the Hi-Quality Tobacco Corporation after the twenty-third of this month."

"You figure that's why they're using the code name Cancer Ward?" Encizo asked. "Because they're sabotaging cigarettes?"

"It's possible," Katz said, nodding. "We all know that professionals don't use obvious code names which might reveal the nature of a secret operation. But most terrorists are only semitrained and semiprofessional. They're more apt to make such mistakes."

"The records we found at the warehouse are proof of that," Manning agreed. "Professionals wouldn't keep such evidence unless there was a good reason. Even then, it would have been written in code or reduced to microdot form."

"Perhaps they wrote everything in French because they believed it would be more difficult to translate," Ohara suggested. "You did have trouble with it, yes? Only Calvin understood some of the words the terrorists used."

"That's because it's written in patois," James explained. "The Haitian Creole language, not European French."

"And Tigershark is a Haitian," Encizo declared, snapping his fingers. "*Cristo.* I should have guessed a connection before."

"There are thousands of Haitian refugees in the United States," Katz said. "It shouldn't be surprising if a few of them happen to be criminals like Tigershark."

"Not just criminals, Yakov," the Cuban insisted. "Jenson said Tigershark always wore a short-sleeved blue shirt and dark glasses."

"That's right," Manning confirmed. "And there were several more black guys dressed the same way at the warehouse."

"That's the unofficial uniform of the Ton Ton Macout," Encizo declared. "The secret police of Haiti."

"I've heard of them," James nodded. "Real sons of bitches. Papa Doc's version of the Gestapo."

"Papa Doc?" Ohara frowned.

"That was the nickname for François Duvalier," Encizo explained. "He became president of Haiti back in 1957. Later made himself president for life in order to insure his absolute authority on Haiti. Duvalier was one of the worst tyrants in history. He set up the Ton Ton Macout to enforce his oppressive rule."

"Yeah," James agreed. "The Ton Ton Macout was part of Papa Doc's method of taking advantage of the widespread belief in voodooism, which is still practiced in Haiti."

"I thought Catholicism was the main religion in Haiti now," Manning said.

"Don't believe it," Encizo replied. "That's a smoke screen by the Haitian government. Voodoo is still the main religion in Haiti."

"That's right," James added. "Catholic saints serve double duty for voodoo gods. Christian symbols are used as magic amulets, and Latin scriptures are combined with juju chants in rituals. Christianity hasn't conquered voodoo in Haiti. It's been incorporated into the old religion."

"How do you blokes know so much about this mumbo jumbo?" McCarter asked.

"Those who practice voodoo don't consider it mumbo jumbo," James said almost defensively. "Any more than Christians or Jews regard their religions to be just superstitions. I know a little about it because voodoo is part of black America. Africans brought to the western hemisphere were denied their freedom, their culture, the right to speak their native language."

"And missionaries tried to force them to adopt Christianity," Katz added.

"Right," James said, nodding. "But you can't force people to give up their old beliefs and religions. Hitler and Stalin proved that. What happened instead was a new religion based on the African juju that also incorporated Christianity and certain European witchcraft practices. Ever hear about voodoo dolls? Sticking pins and thorns into an effigy to put a curse on an enemy started in Europe."

"I'm familiar with voodoo because it's still found throughout the Caribbean," Encizo stated. "It's best known in Haiti, of course, but it's also practiced in some parts of Cuba. There's a form of voodoo called *Obeah* in Jamaica and a similar religion called *Macumba* in Brazil."

"And voodoo is still practiced in the United States," James added.

"Well, I don't claim to know much about it as a religion," Encizo admitted. "But I do know the Ton Ton Macout are the worst kind of stormtroopers. They've been known to commit cold-blooded murder in broad daylight. A couple Ton Ton even beat a victim to death right in front of an NBC cameraman. They didn't give a damn if it got on film or not."

"It sounds like the Ton Ton Macout has probably learned a lot about the value of terror," Katz mused. "The Black Alchemist conspiracy could very well be a scheme by these Haitian butchers."

"The macabre nature of the terrorists and the very title of the Black Alchemists seems to support the theory," Manning agreed.

"Well, their alchemy consists of killer chemicals and their juju sticks fire bullets," McCarter commented. "That's the sort of witchcraft I can understand. Let's find the Hi-Quality Tobacco Corporation and see about performing an exorcism, eh?"

"Don't jump to conclusions, David," Katz said. "The Cancer Ward warning about cigarettes from the Hi-Quality Corporation suggests the place is to be a victim of terrorist sabotage, not an enemy stronghold."

"The twenty-third is tomorrow," Ohara announced. "That means we'd better do something about this newest threat quickly or those cigarettes will already be on the market."

"Yeah," James muttered. "Otherwise a lot of people might find out just how hazardous to their health smoking can be."

13

Phoenix Force arrived in Virginia the following morning. Stony Man computers had discovered the Hi-Quality Tobacco Corporation was located at the outskirts of Richmond. Brognola had arranged for a contact to meet Phoenix Force when its C-130 landed at a small private airfield.

Two men waited at the runway. They had been given a description of the six men who emerged from the airplane. They did not know anything about Phoenix Force or Stony Man. The pair were cutouts, front men used by intelligence organizations as intermediaries. Like most insignificant cutouts, their mission was simple. They were given no details and they asked no questions. No one would have told them the truth anyway.

"*Boker tov,*" Katzenelenbogen addressed the pair. "*Ma shlomkah?*"

"*Ay neni mayven,*" one of the cutouts replied. "*Ani moodabaur rak ahnglit.*"

"Then we'll speak English," Katz told him.

"Your Hebrew accent is very good," the bilingual cutout remarked.

"I've had a lot of practice," the Israeli answered. "You have something for us?"

"Green Chevy van parked next to the lamppost," the man said as he handed Katz a set of keys.

The cutouts walked away. Their job was finished. Phoenix Force found the van. Its six members loaded several long aluminum cases into the vehicle before climbing in themselves.

"Passwords in Hebrew," James mused. "Clever."

"We'll have to come up with something a hell of a lot more clever than that if we're going to stop the Black Alchemists," Manning commented.

"First we have to do something about the Hi-Quality Tobacco Company," Ohara said.

"Cal," Yakov began, turning to James. "You're the chemist. How do you think the terrorists will try to sabotage the cigarettes?"

"I've been thinking about that," James answered. "My guess is nicotine sulfate. It's one of the deadliest poisons in the world. Just a couple drops inhaled with cigarette smoke may be fatal. Possibly just touching the cigarette with your lips is enough. And what's worse, nicotine sulfate is almost impossible to detect in an autopsy of a smoker with traces of nicotine already in his body."

"Is there any way to detect it in the tobacco?"

"A dark-brown liquid mixed in with a bin of tobacco?" James shook his head. "That's the problem. There's no way we can prove sabotage has taken place."

"Then we'll have to do something else," McCarter smiled. "Something a mite radical, eh mates?"

"You have a suggestion?" Katz asked.

"I have an idea, but it's a bit risky."

"All of your ideas are a 'bit risky,'" Encizo declared, rolling his eyes heavenward.

McCarter shrugged. "If it works we'll take care of the poisoned tobacco and possibly drive some rats out of the woodwork as well. Of course, if anything goes wrong, we'll be in a hell of a mess."

"What's new about that?" Manning sighed.

RAFAEL ENCIZO DROVE A FORD PICKUP to the front gate of the Hi-Quality Tobacco Corporation, with Gary Manning and David McCarter crowded into the seat beside him. All three wore white coveralls, gloves, sunglasses and baseball caps.

"This had better work," Manning muttered.

"Nobody else came up with another plan," McCarter replied.

"Somebody should have," the Canadian said sourly.

The security guard who emerged from his shack and approached the truck appeared to be a typical rent-a-cop: elderly, overweight, carrying neither gun nor baton. He was a warm body in a uniform who was at the site only because the company would rather pay minimum wage for token security than higher insurance rates.

"Morning. You got an appointment?"

"Telephone repair," Manning replied.

"I wasn't told nothin' 'bout that."

"Phone lines are down," the Canadian explained.

"I got a call from the main office a few minutes ago."

"It just happened," McCarter told him, concealing his East London accent with a flawless imitation of an American Midwest TV anchorman. "But the lines within the plant aren't affected. Try an outside line. You'll see what I mean."

"Wait here."

The guard returned to the shack and reached for a telephone on his desk.

"I hope Keio cut the right lines," Encizo whispered.

"We'll know soon enough," McCarter said crossly, offended because not everyone shared his faith in the plan.

"I think the guard just wrote down our license-plate number," Manning commented as he watched the old man scribble something on a clipboard.

They had stolen the pickup truck less than half an hour before. There was no need to worry about the license plates because they intended to abandon the truck as soon as possible. The guard walked to the vehicle and held out his clipboard.

"Okay. Sign right here."

Manning used a pseudonym on the log sheet. The Canadian was ambidextrous. His left-hand penmanship looked nothing like his usual right-hand signature.

The guard waved them through.

When they reached the main building, the Phoenix Force trio quickly vacated the cab of the truck. Manning and McCarter set up a tall ladder while Encizo took three utility belts from the back. Each belt had a sturdy screwdriver, a pair of wire cutters and a radio transceiver.

After the ladder was braced against the wall, the three men donned the utility belts. Manning also took a U.S. Army mechanic's tool bag from the vehicle. He and McCarter then scaled the ladder to the roof. They immediately found a trap door and a large metal box with water pouring from its vents.

"Hey, amigo," McCarter said into his communicator. "You read me down there?"

"Loud and clear, amigo," Encizo's voice replied. They addressed each other in this way to avoid using proper names while transmitting. "How's the view up there?"

"Loverly," the Briton stated. "Located the outside vents to the air-conditioning system and an entrance from the roof."

"Okay. Keep me posted."

Manning removed two canvas bags from his tool kit, handed one to McCarter and placed the other within easy reach. The Canadian then extracted a large green canister and put it in front of the air conditioner. The only marking on its surface read CS. Tear gas.

"We're just about ready to start the show, amigo."

"I'm taking a stroll around the plant," Encizo's voice replied. "Plenty of windows. Cartons of cigarettes are stored in the west wing. Bins of tobacco are in the south."

"Christ," Manning complained as he unzipped his bag and removed an M-17 gas mask. "Does he think we've got a compass?"

"Don't worry." McCarter smiled. "I'm a pilot. I've got a compass inside my head."

"Always wondered what you kept in there," the Canadian muttered. "Better get that trap door open."

"Right," McCarter agreed. He spoke into the radio once more. "All right, amigo. Show time."

The Briton and Manning donned gas masks. After checking filters and eyepieces, they exchanged nods to confirm the equipment was sound. Manning then pulled the pin from the canister.

The gray-white smoke that billowed from the device was sucked into the air-conditioner vents. The tear gas quickly circulated through the building. Soon it infiltrated every room in the plant.

McCarter used his screwdriver to jimmy the lock to the trap door. Manning followed him down the rungs of an iron ladder. It led to a catwalk overlooking the cigarette assembly line.

Dozens of workers had already reacted to the tear gas. Shouting and yelling, they pawed at tear-filled eyes and coughed violently as the air-conditioner vents emitted the grayish fog. Glass shattered: Encizo lobbed a gas grenade through a window. More smoke billowed from the sputtering canister.

The employees bolted from the assembly hall and charged from the building, desperately seeking fresh air for their tortured lungs. With apparently no witnesses, McCarter and Manning found a flight of metal stairs and descended from the catwalk.

"Amigos," Encizo's voice called from the Briton's communicator. "I think everybody has abandoned ship."

"The assembly line certainly has," McCarter replied. "What about the packing area and the offices?"

"I lobbed another grenade into the packing section. Everybody hauled ass. Peeked through a couple office windows. Every room looks deserted."

"Bloody good," the Briton declared. "We'll make certain there isn't anybody left inside. You take care of the blokes who've already left. Remember they're innocents."

"I won't forget," Encizo assured him. "Just don't waste any time in there. A police helicopter might cruise by any second and spot the smoke from the plant. *¿Comprende?*"

"We'll wait until we leave to take our coffee break," McCarter promised.

The two Phoenix Force invaders quickly checked the plant. To their relief, all the employees had fled the building. Manning opened his bag and removed four red canisters with timing devices attached to detonators.

"You take care of the packing and storage rooms," he told his partner. "I'll handle the tobacco bins and the assembly section."

"Only one of these per room?" McCarter asked as he took two canisters.

"They're loaded with thermite. This whole building will be in flames."

"Hope it's insured."

"Brognola will make sure the government pays for all damages," Manning said. "They'll rebuild this place and nobody will lose his job. We only have to worry about ourselves. Make sure you set those dials for three minutes. We'll need enough time to get out of here or we'll be roasted alive.''

They quickly put the canisters in place and set the timers. McCarter met Manning in the assembly hall as the Canadian finished preparing the last incendiary. They exchanged nods to confirm everything was ready, then hurried from the building.

They emerged to find Encizo and fifty-three plant personnel in the parking lot. The Cuban's face was covered by an M-17 gas mask. The filters distorted his spoken words, but an M-10 Ingram in his fists helped him gain the cooperation of the executives and employees.

The Hi-Quality Tobacco people, dazed and coughing from the tear gas, offered no resistance when Encizo herded them to the parking lot and ordered them to wait. Nearby was the security guard whom Encizo had handcuffed to the fender of a station wagon.

Manning headed for the stolen pickup truck as McCarter addressed the stunned congregation.

''We've set incendiaries in the plant,'' the Briton declared, still impersonating a Midwestern as he spoke, loud enough to be heard through the M-17. ''In approximately one minute the plant is going to burst into flames. Do not attempt to enter. That would be suicide. You won't be able to stop the blaze. It's thermite. So. . . .''

The whoomp of four mild explosions, tumbling together to make a single terrific blast, confirmed McCarter's statement. Windows popped out as the fierce blaze erupted. People gasped in horror. Encizo held up his machine pistol and they fell silent.

"None of you are in any danger—yet," McCarter assured them. "But stay away from the building."

Manning pulled the truck forward. Encizo and McCarter backed toward it. The Cuban hopped in the back of the rig while McCarter moved to the passenger door.

"Wait until we're out of sight and then get the hell off this property," the Briton ordered before he climbed into the Ford.

"Why are you doing this?" the plant manager demanded. "Who are you people?"

"Militant nonsmokers," Encizo replied.

Manning stomped the gas pedal. The pickup truck shot through the front gate and skidded onto the dirt road beyond.

14

Calvin James and Yakov Katzenelenbogen drove to the site of the Hi-Quality Tobacco Corporation. The building was still in flames. Three fire trucks from the Richmond Fire Department hosed the structure with water, but the thermite inferno stubbornly raged. The firemen could do little but stand by and let it burn itself out.

The plant executives and employees had pulled their vehicles onto the road where they waited for the police to arrive. James parked the rented Pinto behind a trio of squad cars. A uniformed cop quickly appeared at the car door.

"This area is blocked off, fella. Keep moving."

"Henry Albert Kincaid," James announced briskly as he snapped open an ID folder. "Special investigator for the United States Government. Do you intend to stand in the way of the United States Government?"

"Well, uh. . . ." The cop swallowed hard.

"Where's your superior?" James demanded, opening the car door. "We want to talk to someone in authority."

"Yes, sir," the officer nodded.

James and Katz emerged from the Pinto. The Israeli wore a five-fingered prosthetic and pearl-gray gloves. Although it featured a built-in .22 Magnum pistol with a hollow steel index finger for the barrel, the device was basically cosmetic. Unless one noticed that Katz's right hand was unusually rigid, one would not suspect he was an amputee.

Yakov was impressed by the way James had handled the cop. The young black man was a natural con artist, an ability that has limitless potential. The Phoenix Force pair followed the patrolman to a plainclothesman who was wearily questioning the plant manager.

"I'm Lieutenant Cabot," the detective stated.

"Special Investigator Kincaid," James replied. "This is Investigator Silverman. We want to talk to these people about the conditions of their plant."

"The condition of the plant is obvious," Cabot said dryly. "It's burning down. Take a look."

"Exactly," James nodded, glancing at the Hi-Quality Tobacco personnel. "We want to know what fire regulations may have been violated."

"Wait a minute," Cabot began. "What department of the government are you guys with?"

"The Occupational Safety and Health Association," Katz answered, showing the detective a forged ID card.

"Hell," Cabot snorted. "This is a case of arson, for crissake. OSHA doesn't have any jurisdiction here."

"Fire-prevention violations still apply in a case of arson," the Israeli insisted. "If this fire was indeed set deliberately, and this isn't a cover-up for faulty wiring or carelessness."

"Three guys showed up here about an hour ago and set some sort of firebombs in the place," Cabot declared. "Must have used napalm or something because the flames just won't go out. See for yourself. The fire department might as well order their men to try to piss on that building."

"Professional arson?" Katz raised an eyebrow. "Someone must have hired the saboteurs. I wonder what was in that plant that made it necessary to have it destroyed."

"You're suggesting I ordered this fire?" the manager snapped. "You OSHA guys are a pain in the ass. You're nit-picking lice who specialize in making mountains from mole hills. You're only good at checking toilets to see if they flush or maybe measuring the width of snow shovels to make certain they meet federal standards for sidewalk clearing. You clowns try to accuse me of conspiracy to commit arson, and you'll find yourself with a lawsuit on your hands."

"No one is accusing you of anything," Katz assured him. "But what sort of insurance policy does this plant have?"

The manager snarled a string of profanities at Katz. Lieutenant Cabot tried to calm him. James strolled toward the plant employees to get a better look at four young men standing apart from the others.

They had caught James's attention because they seemed oddly nervous. They shuffled their feet as if trying to scrape gum off the soles of their shoes. They wiped their runny noses and chain-smoked. One guy scratched his left arm, which was covered by a long sleeve.

"Gentlemen," James began crisply. "I'm from OSHA. What's your opinion about what happened here today?"

"Uh, I don't know, man," one of the quartet replied. "Just some crazies burned down the place."

"Crazies?" James glared at the man, staring into his eyes. "Pretty clever for crazies. What do you really think?"

"I told you, I don't know."

"You don't think this was done by international terrorists, do you?"

"Look, man," another youth snapped. "We don't wanna talk about it."

"Why not?" James locked his gaze on the second man's face. "Has management threatened you?"

"Hey, Kincaid!" Cabot snapped. "You and your buddy are interfering with our investigation. I don't give a fiddler's damn if you're Feds or not. You can still wait until we're finished asking questions before you start poking around."

"No need to get hostile," James replied. "Mr. Silverman? Do you agree that we can check on this later?"

"I believe so, Mr. Kincaid," Katz answered.

The pair marched to the Pinto and climbed in. James started the engine while Katz took a pack of Camels from his pocket.

"Find anything of interest?" the Israeli asked, lighting a cigarette.

"Maybe," James said. "Those four dudes over

there. They've got runny noses, dilated pupils and itchy feet.''

"What?"

"Most junkies shoot up in their feet these days. Needle tracks are less obvious that way. One fella looked like he still likes to pump dope directly into the arm. I've seen a lot of strung-out heroin freaks, and I'd be willing to bet I just saw four more over there.''

"Well, we know the Black Alchemists were using junkies in Chicago,'' Katz commented, drawing on his cigarette. "I'll contact Keio and tell him to bring the van.''

"Those guys might leave in separate cars,'' James warned. "We'll need more than one tail.''

"The others should be ready by now,'' Katz replied. "They've had time to ditch the truck, change their clothes and join Keio. McCarter has another rental on hand. We'll have an extra tail.''

"I just hope these nerds lead us to some Black Alchemist big shots,'' James remarked.

"That would be nice,'' the Israeli agreed.

15

Colonel Guerre was proud of his Zombie Warriors. The Haitian military commander watched his elite fighting unit train in a dojo at the Black Alchemists' stronghold. The gymnasium was equipped with barbells, weight machines, heavy body bags and assorted karate training gear.

Like the Ton Ton Macout, the Zombies had received a title associated with voodoo folklore. Zombies are the walking dead, corpses animated by the evil magic of a *bocor*, sorcerer.

True believers fear the Zombie. Haitian peasants often sewed shut the lips of a deceased loved one to prevent the corpse from uttering its name if a *bocor* tried to summon it from the grave.

The Zombie Warriors had been Guerre's idea. Cercueil had immediately agreed. They'd selected the members of the bizarre new fighting unit with care. The Zombies consisted of former Ton Ton Macout and Haitian military veterans. Each man had to have good reflexes and physical strength. But the most important qualification was that they believed in voodoo and Cercueil's magical powers.

The Zombies feared Cercueil. If they disobeyed him, the *bocor* might inflict the *tandritanitani*—the juju curse that causes men to waste away and die. Cercueil had made effigies of every Zombie Warrior, using nail parings and bits of hair from each. The subjects believed Cercueil could thrust needles into the figures and transmit injury to them and that they are powerless to defend themselves against such sorcery since they did not have a *houngon*, a practitioner of benevolent magic, to combat the *bocor*.

To the Zombies this fear was very real. They had all heard of the *tandritanitani* striking down healthy men. Some had actually seen this occur in their native Haiti. None of them considered the fact that the success of the curse was psychological. If the mind believes, the body will die.

Their very name reminded the Zombie Warriors of the fate that disobedience would bring. Cercueil could strike them dead and summon their corpses to serve as genuine Zombies if the *bocor* so desired. Thus they trained hard, obeyed every order and felt grateful that Cercueil allowed them to be Zombies in name only.

Although Cercueil was the force that motivated the Zombies, Guerre was their commander. He supervised their training, enforced discipline, delivered orders. They were his men, his special combat team.

Guerre watched the Zombies lift weights and slam fists and feet into the heavy bags and *makiwara*, striking posts. One martial-arts expert skillfully executed a drill with his *nunchaku*, an Okinawan weapon consisting of two oak sticks joined together by a short chain. The *nunchaku* flashed like a propeller, cut rapid figure-eight patterns, and whirled around him with lightning speed.

Another warrior displayed equal skill with another Okinawan karate weapon: the *sai*, a short swordlike device featuring an eighteen-inch center blade and two curved prongs on the quillon or crossguard.

The weapons spun like batons in his hands, as yet another Zombie attacked with a machete. He parried the machete with a quick *sai* stroke, then snared the attacker's wrist with a prong hook. Before the man could attempt to free his trapped arm, he executed a fast stroke with the other *sai*. The blade sliced air next to the aggressor's temple. Had the blow actually struck, it would have cracked the skull.

Guerre had concentrated on training the Zombies in hand-to-hand combat. It was the best way to build confidence and physical endurance. Besides, the stronghold was not equipped for training with rifles, explosives or land-assault maneuvers.

Later Guerre planned to complete their training. Then they would get firsthand experience when they would return to Haiti and conquer the island nation. And that would be only the beginning. Cercueil wanted to rule over only the superstitious peasants in Haiti, but Guerre planned to conquer an entire network of islands throughout the Caribbean.

Cercueil would not approve, of course. This did not worry Guerre. He would simply have to dispose of Cercueil and claim the gods had called his soul to the spirit world.

Guerre realized that seizing control of Caribbean islands could be dangerous. The Falkland Islands and Grenada proved that. He thought Guadeloupe might be safer since it is a French protectorate. The

British and the Americans would not be apt to retaliate if he invaded Guadeloupe.

Would the French think one little island worth protecting? Guerre doubted that, although he was aware
that the French bombed terrorist camps in Syria to
retaliate for the slaughter of their peacekeeping
troops in Lebanon. Maybe Guadeloupe was not such
a good target after all.

Don't get greedy too quickly, Guerre thought.
Worry about one conquest at a time.

"COLONEL," CERCUEIL CALLED OUT as he entered the
dojo. "Come here, *s'il vous plaît*."

Guerre nodded. He followed the leader of the
Black Alchemists into the corridor. Cercueil tapped
the silver skull handle of his walking stick against his
open palm. Guerre recognized the nervous habit.
Cercueil was troubled, perhaps even afraid.

"Our attack force in Springfield was wiped out,"
Cercueil declared. "Worse, a successful raid was then
conducted against Tigershark's headquarters in
Chicago."

"*Merde!*" the colonel gasped. "Was there any record that could link Tigershark's operation to our
base?"

"None of his people knew about us," Cercueil
replied. "Tigershark took orders directly from Manta at Cancer Ward."

"What if they locate Cancer Ward?" Guerre asked
fearfully.

"That's impossible," Cercueil assured him.
"Tigershark didn't even know where Cancer Ward
is. Nothing can connect the two...."

"Cercueil!" Farley Cole shouted.

Rigid with anger, the chemist approached the two startled Haitians. He thrust an accusing finger at the Black Alchemist boss. His hands were trembling.

"You sons of bitches have been lying to me!"

"About what?" Cercueil seemed calm.

"You told me everything was going as smooth as owl shit," Cole declared. "But I just heard a radio message from one of your flunkies at a base called Cancer Ward. For once the transmission was in English instead of that Creole gibberish."

"Really?" Cercueil toyed with the silver handle of his cane. "What was this message?"

"That their local operation had been terminated," Cole answered. "They said the business was burned out."

"The tobacco company," Guerre whispered tensely.

"That's why you wanted me to come up with something to poison cigarettes," Cole remarked. "Guess that's where all that nicotine sulfate wound up. Well, looks like things went sour again. Another failure."

"You're getting too emotional, Cole," Cercueil said.

"I want out," the chemist insisted. "I brewed up your alchemy potions. I did my job, right? Just pay me now, and you guys can have the blackmail money all to yourselves—*if* you ever see a cent of it."

"So you want your reward now?" Cercueil asked gently, turning the death head of his cane.

"I'll settle for $300,000," Cole declared. "That'll be enough for me to get out of the country and set myself up with a new identity somewhere else. You guys can afford that much, right?''

"Of course," Cercueil said, nodding. "And you'll get what you deserve. . . ."

Without warning he yanked the skull handle and pulled a twenty-four-inch steel blade from the hollow cane. Cole's eyes widened in terror. His mouth fell open in mute fear.

Cercueil lunged. The sword pierced Cole's chest, lanced his heart. Cole convulsed at the end of the blade. Cercueil pulled the sword from the deep wound, and Cole dropped lifeless to the floor.

"I wondered when you'd decide this American *cochon* had outlived his usefulness," Guerre commented as he kicked Cole's corpse.

"He was a fool." Cercueil shrugged, then wiped the blade of his sword with a handkerchief before returning it to the cane scabbard.

"What will we do about Cancer Ward?" Guerre asked.

"We can't afford to take any chances," Cercueil replied. "I'll order Manta to pull out immediately."

16

The Black Alchemist base called Cancer Ward was located at a small Virginia farmhouse a few miles south of Richmond. The house served as headquarters and the barn as sleeping quarters for the base security personnel. A grain silo contained an assortment of insidious chemicals waiting to be distributed by terrorist saboteurs.

Between the house and the barn, two tractor trailer rigs were parked. Several men were loading weapons and crates into the trucks when the four junkies from the Hi-Quality Tobacco Corporation arrived. The visitors hastily parked their battered old Ford Galaxy and hurried from the car.

Two black men emerged from the house. They resembled a sinister version of Laurel and Hardy, but there was nothing amusing about the obese Haitian commander and his short wiry partner.

The fat man was a former Ton Ton Macout storm trooper known as Manta. Like other ex-members of the Haitian secret police, he still wore dark glasses and a short-sleeved blue shirt. Manta also carried a .357 Magnum on his hip and a bone-handled bowie knife in a belt sheath.

His diminutive companion, however, was far more

vicious and deadly. Known only as Barracuda, the waspish killer was a cold-blooded psychopath. He carried a 9mm Star automatic in a shoulder holster, a .25 auto in an ankle holster and a straight razor in a neck pouch. A French MAT submachine gun hung from a shoulder strap.

Barracuda's greatest joy in life was killing. He looked forward to it the way a normal man anticipates going to bed with a beautiful woman.

"What are you idiots doing here?" Manta snapped at the four addicts.

"Somebody burned down the plant, Mr. Manta," one of the junkies replied in a trembling voice.

"We already know about that." Manta clucked his tongue with disgust. "We monitor police radio messages. I repeat: What are you doing here?"

"Well, we figured we ought to come here and hide out for a while," another junkie answered.

"Really?" Manta sneered. "Don't you think that will make you appear a bit suspicious? Did you consider the fact someone might have followed you here?"

"Uh, we didn't think . . . ."

"I'm aware of that," Manta sighed. "That would be asking too much of you. I don't intend to waste time listening to you whine. We've received orders to abandon this site immediately. The men are currently taking care of that, and I'm going to destroy any records we won't need at the new site. Never mind where that is. It doesn't concern you."

"What about us? What's gonna happen to us?"

"Barracuda will take care of you," Manta replied

as he patted his companion on the shoulder and walked away.

The scrawny killer immediately raised his MAT subgun, cocked it and opened fire. He giggled as 9mm slugs slammed into the four heroin freaks. Their bodies executed an uncoordinated dance of death, propelled backward by the impact of the deadly spray of bullets.

The French chatterbox was still blazing in Barracuda's fist when a scarlet spider appeared in the center of his forehead. The stringy "legs" were trickles of blood surrounding a bullet hole.

The shot that killed Barracuda had blended with the noise of the MAT. Manta did not realize his chief enforcer had stopped a bullet until Barracuda fell. Manta cried out in alarm and stumbled backward across the threshold of the farmhouse. Another shot erupted and a 7.62mm slug splintered wood from the doorway inches from his head.

"Missed," Gary Manning muttered as he removed his eye from the Bushnell scope and lowered his H&K G-3 SG-1 assault rifle.

"You got the dude with the machine gun," Calvin James remarked by his side as he watched half a dozen armed thugs rush from the barn.

"And we'll all have ample opportunities to get some more," David McCarter said cheerfully.

The three Phoenix Force commandos advanced from a grassy knoll two hundred yards from the farmhouse. Typical of his daring nature, McCarter plunged forward, eager to close in and use his short-barreled Ingram machine-pistol. Manning and James supplied cover fire with their longer-range H&K and M-16 rifles.

Several terrorists fell as bullets thwacked into flesh. The others ducked behind whatever cover they could find and returned fire. Several Black Alchemists used the trucks for shelter, their attention centered on Mc-Carter, Manning and James. They did not realize that three other members of Phoenix Force had chosen to hit the Cancer Ward base from a different direction.

A shadow suddenly fell across three terrorists crouched behind a trailer. Two of them pivoted with a start. A tall dark figure with a fierce Oriental face glared at them.

Silver flashed in Keio Ohara's fists. The razor edge of a *wakazashi* struck one terrorist in the crown of the head. The samurai short sword chopped through hair and bone. Steel split the man's face and cleaved his brain. He was dead before he could squeeze the trigger of the .38 Special in his fist.

The sword kept moving in a single lightning-quick diagonal stroke. Another terrorist tried to swing his .380 Beretta toward Ohara. The Japanese warrior was much faster. His samurai blade sliced through the man's wrist as if it was made of brittle bamboo. A geyser of blood shot from the stump as the severed hand fell to the ground, the Beretta still clenched in its fist.

Ohara executed a rapid cross-body sword stroke. The *wakazashi* struck his opponent in the right rib cage. The *ichi-no-do* cut sliced through bone and innards to split the terrorist's torso in half. The hideous corpse tumbled to the ground, spilling yards of intestines and quarts of bloodied gore.

The third terrorist retreated from the deadly swordsman. Terrified, he worked the slide of a 1911A1 Colt to chamber a round. Rafael Encizo, whose walking stick was already trained on the terrorist, aimed the cane like a rifle and pressed the trigger.

The harpoon bolted from the cane and slammed into the center of the gunman's chest, blasting through sternum bone to pump deadly curare into the heart. Paralyzed by the South American poison, the terrorist stood motionless for a full second before he toppled to the ground, to slowly die.

Encizo joined Ohara at the rear of the trailer. A Ton Ton Macout goon suddenly appeared at the edge of the rig. Since his comrades had been killed noiselessly, the Haitian did not expect trouble. Startled by discovering the two Phoenix Force commandos, the terrorist quickly raised his 'shorty' CAR-15.

Rafael Encizo reacted with the speed and ferocity of a cornered puma. He slashed his walking stick at the Haitian. Wood struck metal forcibly. The cane snapped and splintered on impact. The force of the blow sent the CAR hurtling from the Haitian's grasp.

The Cuban gave his opponent no time to recover. He lashed a boot into the Haitian's solar plexus. The Ton Ton terrorist doubled up in agony. Encizo quickly swung his left fist to the side of the man's head.

The Haitian fell. Encizo immediately pounced on him. Holding the broken piece of cane in both fists, the Cuban raised it overhead. He swung his powerful arms to drive the splintered tip into the terrorist's chest. The results could have been a scene from a vampire movie.

A soul-chilling primal howl burst from the Haitian

as his body convulsed wildly. Clawed fingers raked the ground. Blood from his punctured heart splattered Encizo. At last his body relaxed and accepted death.

The Haitian's scream alerted several Black Alchemist hoodlums behind the other tractor trailer. Three of them cautiously moved forward, guided by their comrade's death cry. Not one noticed Colonel Yakov Katzenelenbogen at the corner of the barn.

"Bonjour, salaud," Katz called softly. Good day, filth.

The trio turned abruptly to discover the muzzle of an Uzi submachine gun pointed at them. Katz triggered his weapon. A volley of 9mm rounds found the human targets. Bodies twitched and jerked. Bloodied corpses tumbled like mannequins. Katz quickly scrambled to Encizo and Ohara.

"The fat man said he was going to destroy their files," the Israeli reminded his partner. "They must be in the house. I'll hold this position. You stop the fat one before he burns the records."

"Hang tough, Katz." Encizo unslung an H&K MP5 machine-pistol from his shoulder.

Ohara nodded. He slid his sword into its scabbard in his belt and readied a .45 caliber M-10 Ingram.

MANTA WAS BETTER PREPARED for the invasion than Tigershark had been. The Haitian's troops might lose their battle with the attackers, but the American CIA would learn nothing from the Cancer Ward files.

Manta opened all the filing cabinets in his office and placed the drawers on the desk. Then he set a crude incinerator in the center of the room. The device was as simple as it would be effective. Attached to a gallon jug containing a solution of gasoline, motor oil and laundry soap was a highway flare with a number-six blasting cap inserted into it. A three-minute egg timer served as detonator.

Manta had no intention of dying in a blaze of glory for the Black Alchemists. Unlike most of the Ton Ton Macout, he had never deluded himself about his former role with the Haitian secret police. The Ton Ton received no financial recompense from the government of Haiti. They allegedly served their country for patriotic reasons.

Manta knew better. The Ton Ton Macout were permitted to steal, rape and murder among the peasant class. They could take what they wanted. Who needs a salary under such circumstances?

A cynical atheist, Manta considered every religion to be utter nonsense. Though he paid lip service to the voodoo gods, he did not believe in them or Maurice Cercueil's fabled powers as a *bocor*. Manta did not believe in an afterlife, only in survival.

He planned to set the timer to the explosive only when he could secure an escape route. The terrorist commander gathered up his M-76 subgun and crept to a window. There was no fighting in progress at the west side of the farmhouse.

Manta hurriedly set the timer and returned to the window. He checked the area again to be sure it was still safe. He smiled. He had found his escape route. The Haitian unlatched the bolt and slid the window open.

The obese terrorist had difficulty squeezing through the narrow opening. Reluctantly he left the M-76 propped against the inside wall in order to accomplish this feat. He was bathed in sweat and breathing hard by the time he crawled outside. He reached across the windowsill to retrieve his submachine gun.

"Freeze, El Gordo," Rafael Encizo's voice ordered from outside. "You'd be a hard target to miss."

Manta stiffened. He held the S&W blaster in his fists and thumbed off the safety. The Haitian remained draped over the windowsill, his upper torso—and the machine gun—hidden from view.

"I'm stuck," Manta lied, playing the only card he had left.

"Bullshit," the Cuban told him. "Slide out slowly and place your hands on the wall."

"I can't get my belly through," Manta said in a strained voice.

He knew many people think fat men are clumsy, stupid and inept. If he could convince Encizo that he was just an overweight oaf, the Cuban might underestimate him. With a submachine gun in his hands, Manta would have little trouble turning the tables were the Cuban to make a mistake.

"I don't have time for this game," Encizo warned.

He lowered the aim of his MP5 and squeezed off a 3-round burst. Nine-millimeter slugs ripped into Manta's lower legs. Bullets sizzled through both calf muscles. The terrorist bellowed in agony and tumbled backward through the window, the S&W subgun still clenched in his fists.

Panicked by pain and fear, Manta swung the M-76 at Encizo. The Cuban would have preferred to take Manta alive, but he had no choice now. He blasted three rounds into the Haitian's flabby stomach and chest. The fat man thrashed about like a beached whale and then lay motionless as death glazed his eyes.

Encizo saw the incinerating device through the window, and dived through the opening. A forward roll carried him to the improvised bomb. The egg-timer dial clicked toward the red arrow that would detonate the contraption.

Although Encizo was not as familiar with explosives as Gary Manning, he had a good working knowledge of demolitions. Fortunately the device was not complicated. The Cuban deactivated it simply by cutting the wires connecting the egg-timer to the flare.

The roar of an explosion beyond the house startled him. He scrambled to a window and looked out. Billows of smoke and assorted debris, including parts of human bodies, spewed from the windows of the barn. Phoenix Force had trapped several terrorists inside and terminated their careers with hand grenades.

"Rafael," Keio Ohara called gently as he entered the room. "I see you also found an entrance to this house."

At that moment the egg timer began to buzz.

"Better than that," the Cuban said. "I found it just in time."

17

Two terrorists ran for the silo, hoping the Phoenix Force assault team would not attack due to the chemicals stored there. They never reached their goal. Calvin James cut them down with a volley of M-16 slugs.

Four Black Alchemist gunmen who had retreated to the upstairs of the house fired at the Phoenix Force commandos outside. Expecting this tactic, Gary Manning had been watching the windows carefully. As soon as the first sniper appeared, he shot him in the face.

Encizo and Ohara ascended the stairs to the second story. They located the remaining snipers and opened fire. Three more terrorists were quickly reduced to inert masses of pulverized crimson-stained flesh.

The entire battle lasted less than seven minutes. Eighteen terrorists had been killed. None were taken prisoner. None escaped. Phoenix Force had been fortunate. They had suffered no casualties or wounds of any kind.

"My God," Calvin James remarked as he joined the others in Manta's office. "We did it again. In Nam I saw some ass kickers, but you guys are really something else."

"What do you mean by 'you guys'?" McCarter said with a grin. "You've been doing your share and doing it bloody well. Sure you were never in the SAS?"

"David's right for a change," Encizo added. "Brognola couldn't have made a better choice for this mission than Calvin."

"Yeah, Katz," Manning began. "Maybe we can talk Hal into letting Calvin stay with the team after this is over."

James resisted the urge to watch the Israeli react. He did not want to risk betraying his own enthusiasm or possibly see disapproval in Katz's expression.

Calvin James had not felt such camaraderie since he was a Seal in Vietnam. He had never really fit in anywhere else. Too levelheaded to endorse the militant honkey haters, he regarded them as just another breed of racist, no better than their white counterparts. Most were just noisy troublemakers who would rather blame everything on whitey than accept responsibility for their own lives.

Yet James was equally contemptuous of blacks who feel apologetic for the color of their skin. Dark pigmentation does not make a man less intelligent, less capable or less human than anyone else. James had no intention of groveling before anyone.

Most of the white community was a pain in the ass. Red-necks judged a man's worth by the shade of his skin. Liberals seemed to feel moaning with guilt over slavery somehow made present conditions better. Both only served to annoy Calvin James.

Extremists, black as well as white, seemed to want

James to fall into some sort of stereotype. The hell with all of them. He did not want to be an Uncle Tom or H. Rap Brown. He did not want to shine shoes for a living and he especially did not want to be hired for a job because Affirmative Action said an employer needed a token black.

Phoenix Force was different. They did not question his ability or treat him as if he had an IQ equivalent to his shoe size. None of the five seasoned combat veterans were concerned about social conscience or petty prejudices or ethnic bullshit of any kind.

The men of Phoenix Force were the best, the very best. And they treated Calvin James as an equal. They respected his ability and intelligence. They praised his courage and combat savvy. James could not imagine a greater honor than to be part of this unique fighting unit.

"We'll see about that after the mission," Katz replied to Manning's suggestion about making Calvin James a permanent member of Phoenix Force.

"Les Quartier de Cancer," a voice called from a large ham radio set behind the desk that had formerly belonged to Manta. *"Répondez, s'il vous plaît."*

"That could be the Black Alchemist high command," Manning declared as he headed for the radio.

"Wait a minute, Gary," Katz urged. "If that's a Haitian on the line, you'd better not answer. Your Quebec French won't pass for Creole very long."

"Neither will our European French," McCarter replied.

"That leaves you, Cal," the Israeli announced.

"I only know a little patois lingo," James confessed. "Hell, I won't be able to fool that guy for long."

"Try," Keio Ohara urged. "Keep him on the radio as long as possible."

"What good will that do?"

"I'll explain later," the Japanese said, surprising everyone with his uncharacteristic gruffness. "Just *do it*."

"Les Quartier de Cancer?" the voice from the radio repeated.

Calvin James hurried to the ham unit and grabbed the microphone.

"This is Cancer Ward," he said in French, trying to imitate a Haitian accent. "Identify yourself, *s'il vous plaît*."

"Identify myself?" The voice sounded stunned. "Are you insane?"

"Just joking, *patron*," James replied lamely. "Papaloi always says we should not lose our sense of humor, *oui*?"

"Qui êtes-vous?" the voice demanded.

"Qui suis-je?" James answered. "I am Henri Assaisonnement. You know me. Everybody in Ton Ton Macout knows Henri Assaison...."

"Imbecile!" the voice snapped. "Don't use your real name on the radio and don't mention the Ton Ton Macout!"

"Why not? You just did."

"Merde alors," the Haitian groaned. "Where is Manta?"

"Manta?" James thought fast. "Oh, he's in the bathroom. Drank some *sousou* when he had a ritual to the *loas* of *Petro* last night. That blood must have come from a sick pig because Manta has had diarrhea...."

The Haitian terminated transmission, evidently not interested in Manta's bowel habits.

"Did I stall him long enough?" James asked as he hung up the mike.

"We'll know after we hear from the Federal Communication Commission," Keio Ohara replied.

"How's the FCC going to help us?"

"The FCC monitors radio broadcasts," the Japanese electronics expert explained. "They are particularly concerned with ham and citizens-band-radio broadcasts that use a power output greater than one-thousand watts."

"If that was the Black Alchemists' high command," Katz mused, "they're probably using a very powerful transmitter—assuming they're located some distance from here."

"I see why you wanted Cal to stall them," Encizo said to Ohara. "The longer the transmission, the better the odds the FCC could trace it."

"I'm certain they've already taken an interest in previous transmissions," Ohara replied. "It is illegal to transmit from one country to another without a special license."

"But the Black Alchemists are probably transmitting from a base somewhere in the United States," Manning interjected.

"True. But they have obviously been broadcasting

in Haitian Creole, yes? Any ham-radio broadcast in any language other than English will certainly be suspected of this violation and thus merit an FCC investigation."

"Then let's contact Brognola and have him check into this," Katz declared. "If everything holds true, we might be able to find the terrorists' headquarters within the next eight hours."

18

"The FBI and local police will be rounding up terrorists from Ohio to Iowa," Hal Brognola declared happily. "Those files from the Cancer Ward base will put the Black Alchemists' entire Midwest operation out of business."

"But it isn't over yet, Hal," Colonel Katzenelenbogen replied as he sat at the conference table in the Stony Man War Room. "We've cut off some tentacles, but we still have to find the head of the giant squid to destroy it."

Phoenix Force had headed straight for Stony Man headquarters after the Cancer Ward strike was finished. The team gave Brognola the files from the terrorist base and a detailed report about the raid. The Fed was delighted by Phoenix Force's progress and excited by the possibility of locating the main headquarters of the Black Alchemists.

For the men of Phoenix Force, the trip to Stony Man allowed an opportunity to rest. In less than forty-eight hours they had been in three firefights and had crushed two terrorist bases. During that time they had been driven by sheer willpower. There had barely been enough time to grab a quick sandwich or a short nap.

As the Stony Man computer complex analyzed the data from Cancer Ward, Brognola contacted the FCC. Phoenix Force retired to guest quarters and gratefully stretched out on bunks to get as much sleep as possible before returning to the war against terrorism.

Katz had been the first to wake. The Israeli never failed to impress Brognola. Yakov seemed to function as well after a two-hour nap as most men who have slept all night. He seemed to have developed a built-in alarm clock. Brognola could almost set his watch by the guy.

"Keio's theory about that broadcast in Creole was right on the money," Brognola told Katz. "The FCC has been monitoring the transmissions for the last two months. Tell Keio he wins a cigar."

"He doesn't smoke," Katz replied dryly.

"I'll smoke one for him," the Fed shrugged. He consulted a printout sheet. "The broadcasts have been sent by a privately owned radio station in the Rocky Mountains. High elevation and powerful equipment. That's how they managed to put out such a long-range signal."

"A radio station?"

"It's owned by a rich Haitian named Maurice Cercueil."

"Rich and Haitian seldom go together," the Israeli remarked.

"Cercueil is an exception." The Fed checked his printout sheet. "He was the chief of the Ton Ton Macout for more than twenty years under François Duvalier. Must have collected a goddamn fortune by robbing peasants of what little they had. CIA also suspects the guy was involved in Caribbean heroin traffic. When Papa Doc died, his son took over Haiti. Guess 'Baby Doc' didn't trust Cercueil because he kicked the old gangster out of the country. . . ."

"And he wound up in the United States," Katz said, completing the statement for him.

"Yeah," Brognola grunted. "Ain't we lucky?"

"I'm surprised Jean-Claude Duvalier let Cercueil leave without relieving him of his ill-gotten fortune."

"I suppose he had some reason," the Fed mused.

"Duvalier couldn't exile Cercueil without showing proper respect to the former head of his father's secret police," Calvin James explained, entering the room. Brognola and Katz turned to face him. "He wouldn't want the new commander of the Ton Ton Macout to doubt the rewards of loyalty. That might cause a mutiny at Port-au-Prince."

"You know about Cercueil?" Brognola asked.

"I've talked to enough Haitian refugees to know Cercueil is a rotten son of a bitch," James said, pouring himself a cup of coffee. "But he's intelligent, cunning and shrewd. The Haitians believe he's a *bocor*, night wizard."

"Night wizard?"

"In voodoo they refer to 'day magic' as good and 'night magic' as evil. Just as Europeans referred to white magic and black magic. Anyway, the Haitians figure Cercueil is the original Midnight Man. Some even say he's Baron Samedi himself. If ever a dude was a prime suspect to be the ringleader of a conspiracy like the Black Alchemists, Cercueil is the one."

"There seems to be little doubt about that," Katz agreed. "But why hasn't the FCC closed down his radio station if he's been violating federal regulations?"

"Cercueil has been charged with the violations," Brognola answered. "But he doesn't seem concerned. The Haitian is difficult to reach. He lives at that radio station on top of a damned mountain, and they don't even have a phone up there."

"His station doesn't take requests?" James grinned.

"As a matter of fact his station seems to concentrate on presenting traditional Haitian music and bilingual news presented in English and Creole," the Fed stated. "Cercueil claims he's presenting a public service to Haitians living in the United States. The bastard's lawyer is even trying to sue the FCC for harassment."

"And discrimination?" James asked.

"Yeah," Brognola admitted awkwardly. "They even got some chicken-shit civil-rights group to make a televised protest about it."

"Some idiots don't think there can be any black good guys," James said with a smile. "And other idiots don't think there can be any black bad guys. I'm not surprised a slick snake in the grass like Cercueil would try to use his skin color for a smoke screen. Letting a creep like him go unpunished sure as hell won't help black people's image."

"Any recon information about the radio station?" Katz inquired.

"We'll have some pretty soon," Brognola promised. "Colonel Roberts of Air Force Intelligence at Lowry Air Force Base near Denver has been assigned to the job."

"Can Roberts set us up with a gunship to transport us to the radio station?" the Israeli asked, inspired with a plan.

"He shouldn't have any trouble with that," Brognola replied. "We can also manage a clearance for whatever weapons and equipment you'll need."

"Fine," Katz nodded. "We can't afford to waste time. The Black Alchemists won't stay at their base for long. They've probably assumed the Cancer Ward operation has been terminated. Basically these terrorists are amateurs and they've made some bad mistakes, but Cercueil isn't stupid. He won't simply wait on his mountaintop for the sky to fall on him."

"I know," Brognola agreed. "But I wish we had more information on that place. Hell, we don't have any idea how many terrorists are located there or what sort of defenses they have."

"That's not a new problem for us." Yakov shrugged. "We'll just have to expect the worst. That way we won't be disappointed."

"If you need additional personnel," the Fed began, "Colonel Roberts is authorized to supply you with as many men as you'll need."

"The fewer involved, the better our security will be," Katz replied. "It's best that Phoenix Force operates pretty much on its own in the field."

"Okay," Brognola said. He turned to James. "Well, Cal, you've been a valuable asset to the unit on this mission. However, I'm not sure we'll need a biochemist for the final strike on the radio station, so we can ship you back to San Frisco today if you'd like.''

"I'd like to see this through to the end, sir.''

"You're pretty much on loan to us from the Frisco SWAT team,'' the Stony Man honcho frowned.

"They can wait,'' James said.

"You feel strongly that you'd like to continue?''

"I do.''

"What do you think, Katz?''

"Everyone on the team would agree that we couldn't have gotten as far as we have as quickly as we have if Calvin James hadn't been with Phoenix Force on this mission,'' Yakov declared. "He has earned the right to be part of the final act.''

"That's all I need to know. You're still on the team, Cal.''

"Thank you, sir.''

"Don't call me sir, for crissake. Nobody uses that term in this room. You guys better get ready to haul ass. Good luck. You're sure as hell gonna need it.''

19

Phoenix Force arrived at Lowry Air Base a few hours later. Colonel Roberts, a stout muscular man with a receding hairline, was waiting for their C-130. He escorted the six antiterrorists to command head-quarters. Once again, Phoenix Force found itself in a military conference room.

"We sent four Huey gunships over the mountain range to observe the radio station," Roberts told them.

"Four?" Rafael Encizo asked incredulously. "That many helicopters must have caused enough noise to give a deaf man a headache. Some covert operation! You've alerted the bastards to expect trouble."

Colonel Roberts tensed with anger, but David McCarter spoke first.

"Take it easy, mate," the Briton told Encizo. "The colonel hasn't made a mistake. The Air Force makes plenty of practice flights over the Rocky Mountains, right? A single helicopter might seem suspicious, but four choppers flying in formation would appear to be another training exercise. No reason for the blokes to get excited about that."

"That's the way we figured it," Roberts replied,

his ruffled feathers slowly smoothing. "I might add that the United States Air Force hasn't failed to notice that radio station until now."

"You've been suspicious of the place in the past?" Katzenelenbogen inquired.

"We've found it...interesting," Roberts answered, choosing the adjective carefully. "Previous flights over the area brought back photographs of armed sentries posted around the station. When we found out it supposedly belonged to that Haitian character, most of us guessed it was a CIA front of some sort. The Company denied it, but you know how intelligence outfits lie to each other."

"I've heard about it," the former Mossad agent said, nodding.

The Air Force colonel continued. "After I received orders directly from a Pentagon source to recon the area, I had no intention of sending just one chopper. I wanted my men to have enough firepower to defend themselves if unfriendlies at the radio station attacked them. God knows what sort of weapons they have hidden at that place. Personally, I don't even know who they are."

"Then your gunships were fully armed?" Encizo asked.

"That's not a breach of security. We often have training exercises with armed aircraft."

"I'm sorry we butted heads, Colonel," the Cuban said. "I just want to reduce my chances of getting killed."

"Perfectly understandable," said Roberts.

"Did all the airmen in those gunships realize they

were on a recon mission?'' Katz asked, forever concerned with maintaining security.

"No. Captain Colton and his crew were the only men who knew the real purpose of their mission. The others thought it was just another training exercise."

"This Captain Colton," Keio Ohara asked. "He's with Air Force Intelligence, yes?"

"Correct," Roberts confirmed. "Colton is probably the best man I've got. He served three years regular Army in Nam. Saw combat as a chopper pilot with the 82nd Airborne. He was also involved in a couple SOG missions over there. Resigned from the Army after the war, but later joined the Air Force Reserves."

"A part-time intelligence officer?" Calvin James asked.

"Not really. True, Colton still works as a civilian helicopter mechanic, but he's on call twenty-four hours a day for the Air Force. He's reliable."

"He sounds fine," Gary Manning pronounced. "Have the photographs taken on the recon mission been processed?"

"I've got them right here."

Roberts placed a briefcase on the table. He worked the combination lock, opened the valise and extracted several photographs, which he handed to Katz. The Israeli examined them and nodded with satisfaction before passing them to the others.

The photos of the radio station revealed a large, flat-roofed two-story building on the summit of a mountain. Two armed sentries patrolled the neighboring cliffs.

"How high is the mountain?" Katz asked, lighting a cigarette.

"Well, it's not exactly Mount Elbert," Roberts replied. "But it's no mole hill either. About six thousand feet."

"Indeed," Ohara mused. "They have to be elevated to transmit radio signals."

"We've picked up their broadcasts before," Roberts commented. "Figured it would be a good test for our translation department. Just about burned out some computer circuits trying to make heads or tails out of that Creole lingo. Hardly worth the effort. Mostly lessons in English, news reports, recipes and stuff like that. Some of the transmissions seemed to be coded messages. That reinforced our suspicion about a CIA front. Maybe a scheme to organize an invasion like the Bay of Pigs."

"Hopefully, the United States will never be involved in another mess like that," Encizo remarked.

"The guards appear to have H&K 33A2 assault rifles," Manning stated as he examined the photos. "Probably they double the sentries at night."

"Better assume they also use infrared scopes after sundown," James added. "What do you figure that platform on the roof is for?"

"Looks like a helipad to me," McCarter answered. "How else would they get supplies up there?"

"Makes sense," Manning agreed. "That means there must be a rooftop entrance. There doesn't appear to be a back door. Just two ways in and two ways out."

"There are windows," Ohara corrected. "However, I doubt that they have an alarm system. The site is located in a desolate area and difficult to reach unnoticed. Also, their electrical power source is limited. Why waste it on security measures that appear unnecessary?"

Encizo stared at the photos, trying to find a clue to Ohara's statement. Finally he asked: "How can you tell the power source is limited?"

"The rectangular panels on the roof," the Japanese electronics expert explained, "are photovoltaic cells used to gather energy from the sun. The station is powered by solar energy. Night generators must be run to charge storage batteries. Assuming they broadcast after dark, with an output of more than one-thousand watts, and that they don't turn off all the lights in the station, there won't be much left for alarm systems."

"I doubt that they have any ground alarms," McCarter commented. "But they might have radar. Perched on top of a mountain, they're probably more concerned with an invasion from the sky."

"You're not planning to launch an air strike?" Roberts inquired.

"There may be information stored in the station that is critical to national security," Katz replied. "We simply can't blow the place to bits with rockets."

"We'll have to climb the mountain," Manning said, frowning. "That means we've got to scale a rock wall six thousand feet high and try to remain concealed all the way to the top."

"Concealment won't be as big a problem as noise," Colonel Roberts said. "You won't be able to climb a mountain that size with just your bare hands. You'll have to use ropes and pitons. If you hammer those pitons into rock, there's a good chance the guards will hear you."

"We can use our nuts," James stated.

"Our what?" McCarter asked in mock horror.

"Did you two rehearse this act?" Katz inquired dryly.

"Chocks and nuts are climbing devices," Manning explained to the Air Force colonel. "They're fairly new tools for replacing pitons. Instead of hammering them into rock, the nuts are wedged into cracks in the rock wall. They're adjustable and easily removed and reusable if needed."

"Best of all," McCarter added, "they hardly make any sound at all."

"It's been a few years since I've done any mountaineering," Roberts admitted. "Your plan seems awfully risky. You'd better hope those sentries don't happen to look down and see you crawling up the face of that mountain."

"We've considered that," Katz replied. "Can you supply us with a chopper and a pilot?"

"I was told to cooperate every way possible," Roberts answered. "You may have Captain Colton and the gunship of your choice."

"We'll just need the whirlybird," McCarter said. "I can fly it."

"We'd better have Colton," Katz told the Briton. "You're our most experienced climber, and you're also our best shot with both a silenced pistol and that Barnett Commando crossbow you're so fond of.''

"Crossbow?" Roberts raised an eyebrow as he looked at McCarter. "SAS?"

"William Tell Association," the Briton replied with a grin.

"I've done some climbing too," Encizo announced. "And my ankle hasn't given me any trouble since. . . well, for a while."

"It'll give you hell if you have to climb a mountain," Yakov told him. "I'm not going to try to scale that rock wall either. That would be asking too much of my prosthetic. Six thousand feet is just too damn many feet for us. But don't worry. We'll still be part of the action."

"And there ought to be plenty of action for all of us," Gary Manning remarked with a shrug.

20

The great rotor blades of the H-34 gunship sliced through air like the scythe of a vengeful Grim Reaper. The transport tipped forward through the twilit sky, flying above Colorado's Uncompahgre Plateau.

"And to your left," Captain Colton called to his passengers, cheerfully imitating a tour guide, "you can see the Haitian American radio station famous for its Creole recipes, *assotor* music and mysterious conspiracies."

Colonel Katzenelenbogen adjusted the light-density level of his Starlite viewer and gazed down at the station. The building seemed ominous, a variation on an Alpine fortress guarded by stormtroopers. The guards were black men, clad in blue windbreakers and dark glasses instead of Nazi uniforms. Yet Katz realized the Black Alchemists were not unlike the swastika-wearing enemy he had fought forty years earlier.

Corruption, greed and evil are universal traits of the dark side of man's nature. Animal Man, as Mack Bolan might say. The brute is found in every culture and every ethnic group. No nationality is free of the savages who thrive on destruction. Regardless of race, uniform or political ideology, the savages are basically the same.

Phoenix Force had been created to combat Animal Man wherever he appears and whatever form he assumes. If civilization is to endure, if it is to prosper and grow, then the barbarians must be stopped.

Until knowledge conquers fear; until understanding replaces extremism; until all people can live in peace without any threat to freedom; there will be a need for Phoenix Force.

"They haven't pulled out yet," the Israeli announced, handing the Starlite to David McCarter. "There are still guards posted around the building and lights on in the windows."

"Bloody place looks just like the photos," the Briton commented as he peered through the viewer. "Thank God for that. I can do without any ruddy surprises."

"I'm sure they've got some waiting for us inside the station," Manning offered.

"I hope they haven't destroyed their records," Keio Ohara remarked.

"Hey, man," the copilot of the gunship said, laughing. "Why would a radio station destroy its records?"

"Can't be sure about that," Calvin James grinned. "The dudes running that place ain't exactly stereotypes."

"Captain Colton," Katz began. "You mentioned a ravine in the area?"

"Yeah," the chopper jockey replied. He reached between his knees for the cyclic control. "I'm taking you there now."

He applied pressure to the cyclic, banking the copter to the right. Colton used the collective to maintain altitude and turned the throttle inboard to reduce speed. McCarter nodded with approval.

"Where is this ravine?" Rafael Encizo inquired.

"About five miles west of your objective," Colton answered. "There's a pass extending back to the enemy base. Can't say how rough it'll be to travel by foot."

"We'll let you know later," Manning told him, checking his Heckler & Koch G-3 SG-1 rifle. Black plastic and stamped steel glinted slightly.

"Better get ready," the copilot advised. "We'll be over the ravine in about ten minutes."

"Right," Katz told his teammates. "Don't forget the communication signals. One beep every thirty minutes to let us know you're all right. Two beeps if you need help and three when you reach the foot of the mountain."

"Simple enough," McCarter replied, adjusting the straps of his climbing harness. "I just hope the bastards don't pick up our frequency."

"That's why we're using signals instead of verbal communication," Manning said. "There's no way we can know the range of the enemy's radio monitors."

"Yeah," James commented as he clipped some chocks and nuts to his hardware sling. "But the sons of bitches might be able to pick up the beeps."

"The transmission will be too brief for them to home in on a location," Ohara stated, sliding his *wakazashi* sword into his utility belt. "The only danger is the signals would appear stronger on their monitors as we approach the mountain. It could warn the enemy."

"We've been over this before," Manning said, sighing. "It's a calculated risk, but there's no way to avoid it. We can't be certain how long it'll take to reach the mountain, so we can't make an accurate estimate. Communications are essential."

"Let's go over this one more time," Katz began. "Mr. Brown?"

"I'm still awake," McCarter said, responding to his most recent alias.

"You're the mountaineer expert," the Israeli stated. "You'll supervise the climb. Mr. Yamoto will be in charge of communications."

Ohara nodded.

"Mr. Green and Mr. Kincaid will be support," Katz concluded, referring to Manning and James. "Any questions?"

"I've got one," Captain Colton declared, his hands still on the controls and his eyes on the instruments. "Do you fellas plan to take any prisoners?"

"That's possible," Katz replied. "But not very likely. I doubt if we'll be able to take more than a few of them alive."

"Good," the pilot stated. "I don't want to overload my chopper. Hold on. We're going down."

Colton applied slow, firm pressure to the collective control. The helicopter gradually descended in a valley shaped by the peaks of four mountains. If the Black Alchemists were watching, it would appear that the gunship had simply traveled beyond the horizon.

The chopper pilot switched on an infrared search

light and continued to lower the H-34 until it was approximately thirty feet from the ground. The surface below was too uneven for a landing, so the chopper had to assume a fixed hover. Colton gripped the cyclic in one hand and the collective in the other to maintain position and altitude while his feet worked the rudders to keep the heading steady.

"Go!" the copilot shouted.

Two cables dropped from the carriage of the H-34. McCarter and James seized the ropes. They descended rapidly, half climbing, half sliding to the ground. Ohara and Manning followed. When all four touched earth, Encizo winched up the cables. The helicopter then rose and disappeared over the summit of a mountain.

"Anybody twist an ankle or puncture a boot on a sharp stone?" James asked. "Don't be a tough guy. If anything like that happened, tell me so I can do something about it before we start our little stroll."

No one had suffered from such minor injuries. The four used flashlights to check their gear once more. You can never be too careful with equipment when your life might depend on it.

In addition to his M-10 Ingram and Browning Hi-Power, David McCarter carried a Barnett Commando crossbow. A modern version of a centuries-old weapon, the Commando featured a skeletal metal stock and a cocking lever so it could be loaded and fired much faster than a traditional crossbow.

Gary Manning had his trusty H&K G-3 SG-1 and the S&W .41 Magnum revolver. He also carried a Corps of Engineer's modified backpack of explosives.

Numerous detonators were in the pouches of a utility vest as well.

Keio Ohara was armed with a .45 MatchMaster pistol and an M-10 Ingram in the same caliber. After he touched ground, the Japanese took the samurai sword from his belt and strapped it to his back. The hilt was positioned at his right shoulder to allow a rapid draw if necessary. Ohara also wore a utility vest that contained several *shaken*, throwing-star weapons employed by practitioners of *shuriken-jutsu*.

Calvin James wore his Jackass Leather shoulder-holster rig with the Colt Commander under his left arm and the G96 knife sheathed under his right. The M-16 assault rifle was slung over his right shoulder and a .357 Colt Python was holstered on his hip. All four men also carried fragmentation and concussion grenades.

They were also equipped for climbing. Each man wore klettershoes, climbing harness and hardware sling complete with carabiners. The spring-loaded D-shaped carabiners are used to connect climbing ropes. They also had plenty of rope, chocks and nuts.

"That's northeast," Manning announced after consulting a compass strapped to his wrist. "That's where our objective is."

"All right, mates," McCarter began. "You've all done some mountaineering in the past, so I won't lecture you about safety, fundamentals and all that rot. Just remember the slab of rock we have to crawl up is about six thousand feet high. We'd better not be dog-arse tired by the time we reach the mountain. So don't try to break any speed records jogging to the site. Save your energy for the climb."

"How do you think we should handle the climb?" James asked. "Follow the leader or leapfrog?"

"Leapfrog," the Briton replied. "That way we'll all take turns route finding and leading. We'll move a lot faster that way. We'll also distribute the physical exertion pretty evenly that way. We'll still have a bloody great firefight to deal with when we reach the top, so we don't want anybody too exhausted to participate in the main event."

"I just hope Katz and Rafael receive our radio signal," Manning remarked. "Colton said he'd land the chopper on a plateau about ten miles from here. That's a hell of a range to transmit with our communicators."

"I altered the transceivers to handle the distance," Ohara stated. "My only concern is that the surrounding mountains might block our radio waves. There's also the possibility that the enemy may be able to jam our frequency if they pick up the beeps on their receivers."

"Why didn't you mention this before?" Manning asked.

"I didn't see any reason to concern you with such matters," the Japanese said sheepishly. "There's nothing we can do about it and we have to accomplish our mission, yes?"

"We might have a bit of trouble doing that without air support," McCarter muttered. "Well, we could stand around here and fret about what might go wrong, but that won't get the job done."

"Yeah," James agreed. "Let's get the show on the road."

21

The path to the mountain was rugged. Frequently the four Phoenix Force commandos encountered piles of boulders, scree from rock slides and blockades more than fifty feet high. Such obstacles made progress difficult, but all four men were in excellent physical condition and determined to carry out their mission.

McCarter, James, Manning and Ohara approached the mountain cautiously. They used the available natural cover to conceal their movement. The radio station at the summit was barely visible, a black sinister shadow atop a great stone monolith.

"So far so-so," Calvin James whispered tensely as they reached the base of the rock wall.

"Yeah," Gary Manning agreed equally quietly. "If they knew we were coming, they probably would have had snipers with infrared sights pick us off by now."

"Unless they're waiting for us to make the climb," David McCarter remarked.

"Uh-huh," James said sourly. "If they've spotted us and they have infrared scopes, they've seen our mountaineering gear. Wouldn't take an Einstein to figure out what we're planning to do."

"I see your point," Manning said. "Why shoot us

when they can just wait for us to climb the mountain and then drop rocks on us?''

"We'll either live or die,'' Keio Ohara whispered. "That is the nature of our karma. We should not fear either fate.''

"I ain't afraid to die,'' James replied. "But I can't say I'm real eager to do it just yet.''

"Come along, lads,'' McCarter said with a smile. "Nothing's more fun than playing tag with the Grim Reaper.''

"Has anybody ever told you you're nuts?'' Manning muttered.

"Oh, yes,'' the Briton answered cheerfully.

"Damn,'' Manning said with a sigh. "You'd better send Katz the final signal, Keio.''

"I already did,'' Ohara replied.

"Good man,'' McCarter said. "Let's get the ropes ready. When we get up far enough to get a feel for the rock, make sure you use the bloody chocks and nuts. We'll all be connected by the guideline so if one man falls he'll pull us all down unless everybody uses their gear.''

The Briton took the lead, locating hand and footholds for the others. Where none existed he used the chocks and nuts. McCarter lodged them into cracks and secured ropes to assist the other climbers.

It was a demanding task. Their lives depended on the strength of their fingers and the grips of their shoes. Most of all, they had to rely on their teammates. All four men had to work together and trust one another. Calvin James once again felt a rewarding sensation in the knowledge that the ultraprofessionals of Phoenix Force trusted him and accepted him as one of their own.

Almost halfway to the top, Gary Manning took the lead. McCarter branched off to the right of the other climbers. Their formation resembled an inverted J as they continued to scale the rock wall.

The sound of stones breaking loose warned James to look down at Keio Ohara at the rear of the formation. A narrow ledge under the Japanese warrior's feet had given way. He clung to the rope with one hand and clawed for a handhold with the other.

"Keio's in trouble," James rasped to Manning.

Ohara found a narrow crack in the rock wall and gripped firmly as his feet pawed for a new hold. Weather-worn stone cracked under his fingers. Ohara clenched his hand into a fist to use as an improvised nut by wedging it into the crack. He hissed through clenched teeth as his body swayed at the end of the guideline.

James and Manning grabbed the line; McCarter was not in a position to assist. The black man and the Canadian pulled in unison. They hauled Ohara upward to the chocks and nuts already secured to the mountain. The Japanese clung to the new position. He looked up at his partners and nodded.

"He's hurt," James whispered to Manning when he saw Ohara's left hand. The glove was torn and stained with blood.

"I'll lead for about another thousand feet," the Canadian stated. "Then you take the lead to the top. Okay, Cal?"

"Sounds good."

Manning was the most muscular member of the team. He possessed more physical strength and endurance than McCarter, but lacked the Briton's climbing expertise. Thus they made slow, steady progress under the Canadian's leadership.

With less than one thousand feet to the summit, Calvin James took the lead. Manning moved closer to McCarter; the climbers now formed an inverted L. The reason was to allow all four to reach the top at roughly the same time.

They continued to climb. The lip of the cliff above seemed to beckon Calvin James. It dared him to touch it. He resisted the urge to rush. His teammates' lives depended on how well he secured handholds and footholds for the others. The placement of chocks and nuts was crucial. James fully appreciated the additional strain McCarter and Manning had endured when they led the team during the bulk of the climb.

The distant roar of rotor blades arrested James's attention. He glanced over his shoulder and strained his eyes to try to locate the black insect that hovered in the night sky.

Katz and Encizo had received the signal. They were heading for the mountain. Colton was flying the gunship with infrared lights only. The H-34 was a warrior shadow, a Viking ghost ship flying into battle.

"Let's move," McCarter growled. "If we're not on the summit by the time the chopper arrives, the enemy will have a bloody good chance to shoot it out of the sky."

There were only a couple of hundred feet left to climb. All four men scaled the mountain with greater speed. Their desperation to reach the top increased when they heard startled voices shout in patois.

"Sons of bitches have spotted the chopper," James hissed under his breath as he clawed at the rock like an enraged leopard.

Suddenly he found himself gripping the lip of the cliff. He stared up at the towering figures of two Black Alchemist sentries, their legs resembling tree trunks as they stood less than a yard from James's position. Both men were gazing at the sky, following the progress of the approaching gunship.

Calvin James silently hooked his left forearm over the cliff and braced his weight across it. His right hand reached for a weapon. The Colt Commander was blocked by the cliff and the M-16 would be too awkward for such close quarters. He decided to draw the .357 Magnum.

"Merde!" one of the Ton Ton Macout guards exclaimed when he glanced down at the intruder.

He lashed a boot at Calvin James's unprotected skull. The ex-SWAT cop weaved his head to the side. The kick grazed his cheek, splitting skin. James ignored the pain and swung his right hand at the attacker's ankle.

James snared the Ton Ton's pant cuff and pulled forcibly. The sentry shrieked when he lost his balance and plunged headlong over the cliff. His bone-chilling howl echoed softly through the night air as he fell to earth six thousand feet below.

"Oh, shit," James gasped as his feet slipped.

He seized the cliff with both hands. James clung to the rock as he kicked wildly, his boots struggling to find a foothold.

With a triumphant sneer the second sentry observed James's plight. The Haitian aimed his H&K 33A2 rifle at the intruder and prepared to squeeze the trigger, his knuckle whitening.

A projectile hissed. Sharp steel struck the sentry under the chin. The bolt punctured flesh at the hollow of his jaw. Flashing upward through the roof of his mouth, it pierced his brain. The H&K fell from uncaring fingers. The man feebly reached for the short feathered shaft that jutted from his jaw, then seemed to melt into the rocks.

His heart racing, Calvin James hauled himself over the edge of the cliff. Sweat soaked his ebony skin. He breathed deeply, grateful to be alive. The dead sentry lay before him, the crossbow bolt buried under his chin. McCarter scrambled over the top, his Barnett Commando clenched in one fist.

"Thanks, man," James told him. "Looks like I owe you another one."

"We don't keep track of that sort of thing," the Briton replied as he worked the cocking lever of his crossbow.

Two more terrorists appeared, one from each side of the radio station. Both wielded assault rifles, swinging them toward James and McCarter. The *phut-phut-phut* of a 3-round burst from a silenced firearm erupted. One of the sentries screamed and fell.

Gary Manning had mounted the cliff. He lay in a prone position, H&K SG-1 held to his shoulder. A wisp of smoke curled from the muzzle of its sound suppressor.

Before the fourth sentry could fire, Keio Ohara's

arm swung like a catapult. A metallic disc whirled through the sky and slammed into the terrorist's face. The man's eyes rolled upward as if to examine the *shaken* star buried in his forehead. He tumbled over the ledge and fell off the cliff. The terrorist did not scream. He was already dead.

Although none of the sentries had fired a single shot, the Black Alchemists inside the building had been alerted of the assault. Perhaps someone heard one of the screams. Perhaps a radar screen had warned them of the approaching gunship.

Phoenix Force was not concerned with the reason. They were too busy staying alive when a flood of terrorists poured out of the radio station carrying an assortment of weapons. Some wielded pistols or shotguns. Others held machine pistols or assault rifles. Few, however, managed to fire a single shot.

Phoenix Force hit the terrorists with its own form of alchemy that transforms human beings into bloodied corpses.

James, McCarter, Manning and Ohara opened fire with their weapons on full auto. Terrorists ran straight into a tidal wave of burning lead. Black Alchemists twisted and hopped from the multiple impact of slugs. Half a dozen crumpled to the ground. Others dashed for cover at the edge of the building.

To their horror, they discovered an H-34 gunship waiting for them. Captain Colton kept the helicopter hovering steadily beyond the building while Rafael Encizo and Katzenelenbogen operated a M-60 7.62mm machine gun mounted at the open door of their transport. They sprayed the terrorists with a volley of sheer devastation. Black Alchemists slumped into bullet-torn lumps.

McCarter and Manning hurled concussion grenades at the closest windows. Glass shattered and the minibombs landed inside the building. A Ton Ton Macout goon reached for one of the grenades. It exploded in a brilliant blue-white flash before he could toss it outside.

Two blasts exploded like giant flashbulbs. Glass burst from window frames. Clouds of plaster dust spat from the gaps. Dazed terrorists stumbled amidst the artificial fog within the radio station clutching heads, moaning from the pain of shattered eardrums.

"That ought to soften them up a bit," McCarter announced, shoving a fresh 32-round magazine into his Ingram.

"Yeah," James agreed as he worked the charging handle of his M-16, chambering a fresh round. "Let's take care of what's left."

"Don't get overconfident," Manning warned. "This battle has just begun, my friend."

22

Captain Colton navigated the H-34 over the roof of the radio station. The gunship hovered above the building. Colton breathed hard, like a weightlifter straining under a heavy burden. Hovering over an enemy site meant exposing the vulnerable undercart of the helicopter to possible attack. Colton had to control the tension to keep his hands and feet steady on the equipment.

"Go!" the copilot shouted to the remaining passengers.

Yakov Katzenelenbogen and Rafael Encizo descended from the chopper, slithering down cables like misshapen spiders to the roof below. Both men were armed to the teeth. Katz carried his Uzi submachine gun and the .357 Eagle in shoulder leather and a Sig-Sauer P-226 pistol on his left hip. An excellent 9mm pistol, the P-226 featured a 15-round mag for plenty of firepower.

Encizo carried an Uzi and a 9mm Model 59 Smith & Wesson—a double-action autoloader that has a 15-round capacity. The Cuban's favorite weapons were in their usual place: a Walther PPK in a shoulder holster under his left armpit, a Gerber Mark I fighting knife clipped at the small of his back. Both men were also burdened with grenades and spare magazines for their weapons.

On the roof, the pair scrambled to a trap door between the copter pad and the solar cells. Encizo drew a steel jimmy from his utility belt and pried at the door until its latch broke. The Cuban opened the hatch and discovered an iron ladder that descended to a corridor inside the building.

Encizo went down, the Uzi clenched in his right fist. Two gun-wielding terrorists saw him and turned their weapons toward him, but Encizo's submachine gun spoke first. Half a dozen 9mm slugs sent the Black Alchemist goons hurtling across the hallway. They collapsed in a corner, their bodies striped with crimson.

As Katz descended Encizo watched for more gunmen. He did not see a door silently swing open next to the ladder, or notice as a tall thin figure emerged, drew a revolver from his belt, aimed it at the Cuban's exposed back.

But Katz saw. Still clinging to the rungs, he lashed a boot into the enemy gunman's face. The man fell to the floor. Yakov jumped from the ladder onto the terrorist's chest, his heels stomping the man's rib cage. Bone cracked and caved in from the impact, driving sharp shards into the would-be assassin's heart.

"There's a flight of stairs at that end," Encizo said, gesturing with his Uzi muzzle toward the west wing of the corridor. "Shall we see if our friends need some help?"

"Let's make certain there aren't any more terrorist

roaches in the woodwork on this floor first,'' Katz replied as he cautiously approached the door from which the gunman had come.

"What's in there?'' Encizo asked when the Israeli peered into the room.

"A bathroom. Presently unoccupied.''

"I wish I had time to use it.''

A metal door at the opposite end of the corridor burst open and the snout of a machine pistol poked around the edge. Katz and Encizo dropped to the floor as the weapon blazed a hasty burst at the pair. Bullets struck plaster and bored into the wall above the Phoenix Force warriors. A blizzard of white dust and chips flew out.

"That room *is* occupied,'' Encizo said softly.

The machine-pistol muzzle retreated from the open door. Encizo and Katz slowly got to their feet, weapons trained on the gunman's position.

"Careful, Rafael,'' Katz warned. "They might be baiting us. Expect a trap.''

Suddenly billows of gray smoke poured from the open door. Tear gas! The choking, irritating mist soon filled the hallway.

Encizo covered his nose and mouth with his left hand and braced the stock of his Uzi against a hip. With his hands full, the Israeli was forced to endure the gas without any form of protection.

Two shapes hopped out of the room. The terrorists resembled monsters from Greek mythology, their faces covered by M-17 gas masks with bug-eyed lenses and hoglike snouts. Both dropped to a kneeling stance and brought the wire stocks of M-76 subguns to their shoulders.

The terrorists made two mistakes. They overestimated the advantage created by the gas, and they spent a crucial second trying to aim their weapons, an all but impossible feat while wearing gas masks.

Katz and Encizo wasted no time. They opened fire the moment they saw the ominous shapes of the Black Alchemist enforcers.

The terrorists were cut down like wheat before a threshing machine. As soon as they fell, Encizo took a concussion grenade from his belt and pulled the pin.

The Cuban dashed to the door. Eyes blurred by tears, he tossed the grenade into the room. Then he pressed his back against a wall, covered his ears with both hands and screamed. Katz followed his example to prevent his eardrums from being damaged.

The blast seemed to shake the entire building. A man's shriek blended with the echo.

Coughing and wheezing from the tear gas, Encizo and Katz dragged the two dead terrorists to the wall behind the door, and hastily removed the M-17 masks. Semiblinded by their watery eyes, the pair inspected the masks by touch more than sight.

"*Mierde,*" Encizo rasped when he discovered a bullet-shattered filter and broken eye lens. "This mask is shot. . .literally."

"I'll try to get you another one," Katz replied.

The other M-17 had not been damaged. Katz slipped it on, pulling the strap to the back of his head with the hooks of his prosthetic device. Katz gathered up his Uzi and headed for the door.

A canister of CN-CD tear gas stood at the threshold, jetting out clouds of noxious fumes. Two terrorists lay senseless on the floor. A third was on his knees, hands clasped to the sides of his dazed head. An M-17 mask concealed the man's face. He was rocking with silent pain.

Katz was surprised by the dazed man's clothing. He wore a replica of a United States cavalry blue dress uniform with silver eagles on the shoulder boards. The Israeli would later find it was Colonel Guerre, second in command of the Black Alchemists.

But at this moment the room itself intrigued Katz more than the oddly dressed disabled terrorist. A bulky short-wave radio sat in one corner and an IBM computer dominated the center of the room. A large map of the United States hung on a wall. Colored flags pinned to the chart most likely represented target areas.

"Their files must be here," Katz exclaimed with relief. "Thank God."

Guerre gazed at the Israeli. He yanked his hands away from his ears and snatched for the .45 on his hip. Katz rushed forward and swung his Uzi at the terrorist's skull, hoping to take him alive. Guerre reacted like a cornered cobra. He struck, his arms rising rapidly to block Yakov's attack.

The Israeli was taken by surprise by the wounded Haitian's speed and strength. Guerre grabbed the Uzi, pulling Katz off balance. Yakov, unprepared for the sudden jerk, automatically pulled back. But there was no resistance. Instead, there was a shove. He went over backward landing on his back with a painful whack.

Tear gas in his lungs had weakened the Israeli. The

Black Alchemist commander leaped onto Katz's chest and straddled it. He pinned Yakov's left arm under a knee and shoved the steel frame of the Uzi under Katz's chin.

The Phoenix Force veteran felt the terrible pressure jabbing into his throat. Guerre was trying to crush his windpipe. Katz realized it would be pointless to attempt to wrestle with his opponent. The Haitian was larger, stronger and younger than the one-armed Israeli. Katz had to do something fast or die. And he had to do it right the *first* time.

Yakov raised his prosthetic and thrust the hooks at Guerre's face. The sharp tine of a steel prong hit the terrorist's gas mask. An eye lens cracked. Guerre screamed as the metal stabbed mercilessly into his eyeball. Katz shoved hard. He drove the hook deeper and deeper, piercing inside the eye socket to the Haitian colonel's brain. Between the two, the horrible fight was silent. Guerre's jaw hung down in a silent, unending scream. Blood filled the eyepiece and trickled over the cracked glass.

"Yakov?" Encizo called as he stumbled into the room, half-blind from the tear gas. "Are you all right?"

"Yes." The Israeli pushed Guerre's dead weight off his chest. "Don't use this fellow's gas mask. It has a hole in it." He wiped the prosthetic on Guerre's mock uniform and polished the tip on the Nazi insignia stitched to the tunic.

THE OTHER MEMBERS OF PHOENIX FORCE had charged through the main entrance of the building. They entered the lobby. Dazed and unconscious terrorists littered the floor.

Several Black Alchemist gunmen were still on their feet. Blood streamed from their ears and nostrils, but they still had some fight left despite their exposure to the flash-bang concussion grenade blasts.

They fired. McCarter and Ohara hit the floor, rolling in opposite directions. James and Manning supplied cover fire from behind. The terrorists were taken off guard when their targets suddenly scattered. Some used their weapons too quickly and failed to aim. Others hesitated a moment too long. Survival seldom accepts compromises. It demands precision.

Manning's H&K rifle and James's M-16 delivered high-velocity hellfire. Three Black Alchemists tumbled to the floor. A fourth swung his M-76 chattergun toward the pair. McCarter and Ohara hit him with a double dose of Ingram slugs that kicked him backward six feet and tore his chest apart.

"Look out!" James shouted when he saw a gunman dressed in Ton Ton Macout fatigues emerge from a room in the west wing.

The killer aimed an MAT submachine gun at McCarter. James quickly blasted a trio of 5.56 mm missiles into the Ton Ton's upper torso. The Black Alchemist hoodlum collapsed against the door, forcing it open. A hand reached for the knob to close it, but fearfully retreated rather than risk attack.

James and McCarter dashed for the room. Ohara headed for a flight of stairs leading to the second story while Manning turned his attention to another door in the east wing. The Canadian aimed his SG-1 rifle at the door that had opened a mere crack.

A projectile struck Manning's backpack. He heard the report of a pistol as the slug tunneled through the plastic explosives in the pack. Composition Four is extremely stable and cannot be detonated by a bullet. The C-4 served to slow down the 9mm round but did not stop it.

The bullet slammed into Manning's left shoulder blade. The impact knocked him to the floor. The Canadian landed hard and did not stir.

Keio Ohara spun about. He saw Manning fall and spotted the Black Alchemist gunman who had shot him. One of the victims of the concussion grenades had recovered consciousness and pulled a 9mm Star automatic from his belt.

The terrorist swung his pistol at Ohara and squeezed the trigger as the Japanese fired his M-10. The gunman's bullet, a 115-grain full metal jacket flat-nose slug, ripped into Ohara's belly. At the same instant, three .45 rounds shattered the Black Alchemist's skull. Blood and brains sprayed over the floor as the terrorist's body thrashed and kicked its death throes.

Ohara groaned. His body jackknifed from the burning pain in his bullet-punctured stomach. Fortunately for Ohara, the bullet bored through his abdomen neatly and without mushrooming. He fell to his knees. He tried to stand, tried to control his breath, tried to conquer the pain. The molten lead inside him flared into a sunlike furnace. His strength faded rapidly. Nerve endings seemed to be scorched by fire. Ohara's body shrieked. It begged him to surrender consciousness.

"*Ee-ya!*" a voice snarled.

Keio Ohara glanced up to see a monstrous shadow rush forward, and the flash of polished steel. The Ingram was smashed from Ohara's hand. His index finger, caught in the trigger guard, snapped like a cheap pencil.

A Zombie Warrior swung the *nunchaku*, aiming for Ohara's head. Two decades of martial-arts training had already motivated Ohara's reaction. Conditioned reflexes took control of his pain-racked body as he instantly rolled away from the assailant. The *nunchaku* struck the floor instead of Ohara's skull.

Two Zombie Warriors had been training in the dojo, the gymnasium, when the attack occurred. They had been spared from the concussion blasts by retreating there when the grenades were lobbed into the lobby. However, they did not have fast access to firearms. They waited for a chance to attack the invaders with their karate weapons. The wounded Ohara seemed a perfect target.

A *sai* spun in one warrior's fists as he moved toward Ohara. The other closed in quickly and whipped the *nunchaku* across the Japanese commando's lower back. Ohara grunted in pain while the first aimed the points of his *sai* and lunged for his opponent's eyes.

"*Haaii-ya!*"

Ohara's battle cry filled the lobby. It was a cry filled with pain and fury. He bolted away from the *sai* thrust and pivoted on one knee to face his assailants. The *nunchaku* whirled again and Gaston prepared another *sai* assault.

Ohara's hand streaked to the haft of his *wakazashi* short sword. Samurai steel slashed as the *nunchaku* swooped toward his head. Metal met wood. Six inches of oak hopped from the *nunchaku* when the blade sliced through one of the sticks. It fluttered away, out of balance.

Ohara spun on his knee to continue the sword stroke. One of the Zombies retreated from the flashing wakazashi. The Phoenix Force fighter corkscrewed to a standing position, his sword held ready in a two-hand grip. Blood welled from the bullet hole in his stomach, but Ohara's face was a samurai battle mask of fierce determination.

The Zombies glanced at each other and exchanged nods. They attacked in unison. The damaged *nunchaku* swung high while the *sai* lunged for Ohara's torso. The Japanese dodged the first weapon and turned to block the *sai*. Steel rang against steel. The sword met a *sai* blade. The other weapon found flesh. The point pierced Ohara's left bicep, gouging muscle and scraping bone.

The pain was terrific. Ohara's scream expressed less agony than fury. A last squirt of adrenaline surged through his system. He raised his sword sharply and rammed the *kashira* butt of the pommel into one attacker's mouth. The blow splintered the Haitian's upper jaw. He staggered backward, stunned and bleeding.

The other lashed the *nunchaku* at Ohara's right temple. The stick weapon missed its mark, but struck a glancing blow to the crown of the Oriental's skull. Keio Ohara did not even flinch. The adrenaline now held full sway.

He suddenly executed a cross-body sword stroke. The *wakazashi* hissed, a bolt of silver lightning wielded by a warrior Zeus. Sharp steel cut into the side of the terrorist's neck. It sliced through tendons and vertebrae, then on to nothingness. His head fell and rolled across the floor like a gruesome giant marble.

The Zombie indeed became a walking corpse. His decapitated body stumbled awkwardly around the room as blood fountained in a deep red rush from the stump of its neck. The Haitian's knees buckled and the hideous apparition crashed to the floor.

Ohara pivoted to deal with the living Zombie. However, even a samurai is not immune to the effects of pain, fatigue and the loss of blood. Ohara was not fast enough to parry the *sai*.

The Haitian's left-hand weapon trapped the samurai sword between its center blade and a hooked tine. Ohara tried to block the *sai* with his other fist, but his wounded left arm was all but useless and refused to cooperate. The enemy swordsman thrust the point of the *sai* into Ohara's solar plexus.

Steel pierced the Phoenix Force commando's chest cavity. He cried out, no longer able to restrain his agony. His attacker smiled and shoved the *sai* deeper. Ohara's blood splattered upon the other's fist and forearm.

The samurai sword fell from Ohara's grasp. Suddenly his arm rose. Ohara's hand executed a fast *hiraken* panther punch. He pumped his last burst of strength into that final, desperate karate stroke. The semiclosed fist struck the terrorist in the throat. Knuckles smashed into the Zombie Warrior's windpipe and crushed his thyroid cartilage.

Ohara and the terrorist fell together. The Phoenix Force commando watched his opponent twitch feebly. The Haitian clawed at his wrecked throat as his heels drummed against the floor. His convulsions soon ceased and all life left his body. The Japanese nodded in grim satisfaction.

Then Keio Ohara's heart stopped.

The pain abruptly vanished. He closed his eyes and peacefully accepted the final judgment of death.

UNAWARE OF THE PLIGHT of their fallen comrades, Calvin James and David McCarter scrambled to the room in the west wing. The corpse of a slain terrorist still lay across the threshold.

The black commando stood behind the open door. McCarter, armed with the compact Ingram, dived to the floor and rolled to the opposite side of the doorway. No shots were fired at his hurtling form.

"You get one chance," James shouted. "Either throw out your weapons and surrender or we toss in the hand grenades."

"This is a chemistry laboratory," a trembling voice replied from within. "I've got potassium chlorate, magnesium sulphate and white phosphorus in here. You know what that means?"

"Yeah," James answered. "It means you'll go up like a Roman candle, fella."

"And you guys will go with me!" the terrorist shrieked.

"Sounds like an American," McCarter whispered to James.

"And he said *I* instead of *we*," the black fighting machine added. "He's probably alone in there."

"Ten to one he's a chemist on their payroll," the Briton commented. "Not likely he's eager to die for the cause."

"Sure doesn't sound like it," James agreed as he put down his M-16. "I've got a plan. Just in case we have to do any shooting, better stick to handguns. I don't think he's lying about the explosive chemicals in there."

"Right," McCarter said, drawing his Browning Hi-Power.

"Hey, turkey," James called to the terrorist. "We figure you've had enough time to decide. Say your prayers, chump, 'cause we're all gonna meet our Maker together."

The black commando tossed an M-26 hand grenade across the threshold. He heard the lone terrorist scream. Shoe leather scrambled across tile. McCarter dashed into the room. James stayed by the doorway, the Colt Commander Combat ready to supply covering fire.

"I've got the bugger," McCarter announced cheerfully.

He had easily found the terrorist. A young black man clad in a white lab smock was huddled in a corner with both hands wrapped over his head. McCarter approached the frightened youth and pointed his Browning at the man's head.

"Just place your forehead against the wall and put your hands at the small of your back, lad," the Briton instructed.

"What?" The terrorist gazed up with a confused expression on his sweat-soaked face. "How...? The grenade...."

"The bloody pin wasn't pulled, you idiot," McCarter growled. "Now do what I told you before I get annoyed and decide to kill you."

"Okay, mister," the man hastily agreed. "Don't do nothing radical."

"Lord love a duck," the Briton snorted. "You're a dandy excuse for a terrorist. Whatever happened to all that rot about dying for the revolution?"

"Look," the youth said. "I'm just a chemist."

"So all you did was help make poisons for Cercueil and company to use to kill innocent people," James said dryly, holstering his Colt.

"They made me do it, man. I didn't want to, but they...."

"Sure," James snapped. "They made you take the money too. Save it for your trial, kid. Where's Cercueil?"

He bent to retrieve his M-16. Then the object of his question suddenly materialized in the hallway. A sinister figure dressed in black with a top hat perched on its head stood before Calvin James. Light danced along the naked blade of the cane sword in his fist.

James grabbed the M-16 as the Haitian master criminal slashed a vicious sword stroke at his face. James dodged the flashing steel, the assault rifle in his fists. Cercueil lunged like a veteran fencer, aiming the sword tip at James's heart.

The aluminum receiver of the M-16 blocked the blade. Cercueil hissed and immediately swung an overhead stroke at James's head. The rifle rose to check the attack. Steel clanged harshly against steel. James quickly swung a heavy boot into his opponent's abdomen. Cercueil grunted and stumbled backward.

James reversed his grip on the M-16, trying to point the rifle at Cercueil and insert his finger into the trigger guard. The Black Alchemist uttered an obscenity in patois and executed a sword thrust toward James's throat.

The black warrior weaved away from the blade. It stabbed the empty air less than an inch from his left earlobe. James quickly raised the barrel of his M-16. Steel struck steel once more. He shoved hard and pushed the blade toward its wielder.

''No!'' Cercueil cried out when he realized what was about to happen.

James fiercely pressed the rifle downward in a hard diagonal stroke. The violent motion shoved the edge of the sword into the side of Cercueil's neck. The Phoenix Force combat champ revolved his shoulders and twisted his trunk sharply. This dragged the blade across Cercueil's throat.

Blood gushed from the horrible wound. The Black Alchemist boss stared at James, his eyes filled with astonishment and sheer terror. Calvin James spat in Cercueil's face and suddenly delivered a furious butt stroke to the Haitian's skull.

The blow almost decapitated Cercueil. Flesh ripped and the tear in his throat widened. The Black Alchemist's head snapped backward and recoiled. Suspended by strands of skin and muscle, it drooped against his shoulder blades. Maurice Cercueil fell. He landed on his back, but his face struck the floor first.

"Jesus, Cal," McCarter remarked as he escorted the prisoner from the lab. "You sure know how to hurt a guy."

"Are you two all right?" Rafael Encizo called as he approached the room.

"A hell of a lot better than most people around here," James replied.

"I noticed," the Cuban said, glancing at the grisly remains of Cercueil.

"Did you and Katz take care of everything upstairs?"

"Yeah." Encizo's expression was grim. "We've got casualties."

"How serious?" James asked, reaching for his medical kit.

"Gary's been wounded," Encizo replied. "And Keio. . . Keio is dead."

The taste of victory suddenly seemed very bitter indeed.

23

"The records you found at the Black Alchemist headquarters have been turned over to the Justice Department," Hal Brognola said to the men of Phoenix Force in the Stony Man War Room.

Five solemn faces gazed up at him from the conference table. Brognola realized they had suffered a great loss. One of their own had fallen in battle, never to rise again.

"The Black Alchemist conspiracy has already been crushed," Brognola continued. "Federal and state authorities are rounding up the remnants of the organization. The President wants me to congratulate all of you on a job well done."

"Thank him for us, okay?" said Gary Manning.

"How's your back?"

"Just a little sore," the Canadian answered. "The bullet was slowed by my backpack. It barely broke the skin. All I got was a bruised shoulder blade. The terrorist probably would have finished me off if Keio hadn't been there."

"He was a damn good man," Brognola stated.

"One of the best," Rafael Encizo agreed. "Hell, they had to shoot him, stab him and club him before he'd go down. Even then, Keio killed them before he died."

"The last thing a man does is die," David Mc-Carter mused. "We'll be lucky if any of us carry out our final act as well as Keio did."

"Have you seen to the cremation?" Yakov Katzenelenbogen inquired quietly.

"Already done," Brognola replied. "The ashes will be sent to his family in Japan after we've had a chance to pay our last respects to a brave and big-hearted warrior."

"And a good friend," Encizo added softly.

"I have a request, Hal," Katz began. "Is it possible to erect a monument to Keio at Arlington Cemetery?"

"A monument?" The Fed frowned. "Yakov, you realize something like that could jeopardize our security."

"Just a small headstone," Katz insisted. "There's no need to put his name on it. All of us will know who it is for. That's what matters."

"That can be arranged," Brognola said, nodding.

"A one-word inscription would be nice," Mc-Carter commented.

"One word?" Brognola inquired.

"Samurai."

"How right you are, David," Manning agreed.

"You want 'samurai' inscribed on a headstone at Arlington Cemetery?" The Fed sighed. "Hell, I'll see what I can do."

Calvin James had remained silent. Although he too had been touched by the death of Keio Ohara, he did not feel he had a right to intrude on the sorrow felt by the others. They had served with Ohara for three years. James was still a newcomer.

The black warrior regretted this status. More than ever, he wanted to remain with Phoenix Force. James had done well with the team. For the first time he *really* belonged. Even his work with SWAT could not compare to Phoenix Force.

"Okay, Calvin," Brognola began. "You were sort of drafted for this mission. If you want to return to the San Francisco Police Department, we'll understand, but we could sure use you here. Especially now."

"Hal speaks for all of us," Katz added. "We want you to remain with Phoenix Force." James felt a rush of blood suffuse his face. The surface of his eyes prickled and his throat tightened momentarily.

"I can't think of anything else I'd rather be doing," James replied tightly. A smile radiated, starting at the corners of his mouth, and spread across his face.

"I surely can't."

The Gar Wilson Forum

The phrase "mindless act of terrorism" is seen and heard so much these days that we stand in danger of accepting it as commonplace rather than seeing it for what it is—a danger signal warning us of a disturbing and potentially deadly aspect of our world.

Whether they are exploding bombs in crowded department stores at Christmastime—as the IRA did in London during Christmas 1983, killing six innocent people, wounding many more and leaving permanent emotional scars on the psyches of countless families—or throwing grenades into crowded Jerusalem streets, terrorists demonstrate a lack of any sense of humanity or compassion for their fellow man. They are capable of functioning only as mindless and remorseless terror machines.

Terrorists are like termites chewing away at the very foundations of our society. Many are the well-educated products of upper-middle-class families. Yet their politics are obscure. With the SAS, GSG-9 and the Mossad, I had the opportunity to interrogate many extremists. Regardless of their political affiliations, their goals were irrational and unrealistic. Their only consistency, then as now, lay in their unanimous choice of a method for social and political change—violence.

Ours is evolving as a world that lives in fear. A world where the innocent are the unsuspecting prey of the irrational. A world where children become the sport of conscienceless bloodletters. A terrorist does not care about the value of human life or individual freedom. That is what makes a terrorist the most dangerous and loathsome beast in the jungle.

Gar

PHOENIX FORCE

#13 Harvest Hell

MORE GREAT ACTION
COMING SOON!

The KGB is ready to sow a deadly crop. Seeding the air over the cities of the Western democracies with the Proteus Enzyme, which eats its way through the victim's stomach wall, the Soviet terror machine plans to spread mass malnutrition. Their insidious mandate: to starve the citizens of the free world into submission.

The five battle-hardened men of Phoenix Force track the Russian death merchants to a tiny Greek island, where the Stony Man warriors plan to reap their own harvest.

Hell will look like paradise by comparison.

Watch for new Phoenix Force titles wherever paperbacks are sold.

Mack Bolan's

PHOENIX FORCE

by Gar Wilson

Schooled in guerilla warfare, equipped with all the latest lethal hardware, Phoenix Force battles the powers of darkness in an endless crusade for freedom, justice and the rights of the individual. Follow the adventures of one of the legends of the genre. Phoenix Force is the free world's foreign legion!

"Gar Wilson is excellent! Raw action attacks the reader on every page."

—*Don Pendleton*

Phoenix Force titles are available wherever paperbacks are sold.

GOLD EAGLE

JOIN FORCES WITH MACK BOLAN AND HIS NEW COMBAT TEAMS!

Mail this coupon today!